# TARGET MARIE
## A FEW GOOD MEN
### BOOK FOUR

## STINGRAY23

# Author's Copyright

This is a work of fiction. Names, characters, organizations, places, events, and incidents are either products of the author's imagination or are used fictitiously. Any resemblance to actual events, locales, or persons living or dead are entirely coincidental.

Copyright © 2022 Stingray23 ALL RIGHTS RESERVED

No part of this book may be reproduced, or stored in a retrieval system, or transmitted in any form or by any means electronic, mechanical, photocopying, recording, or otherwise, without express written permission of the publisher.

This book is licensed for your personal enjoyment only. This book may not be re-sold or given away to other people.

Editing by: Maria Clark

Formatting by: Jessika Klide, LLC

Published in the United States of America

## What are others saying?

*"Military men ... swoon-worthy spice, what's not to love?"*

— *- USA TODAY* Bestselling Author Xavier Neal

*"Adorable sexy ... just plain fun."*

— -Read All About It

*"Hot ... enjoyable ... blissful ... loved every minute."*

— -Book Bangers Blog

*"Packed with so much action and heat."*

— -Within The Pages Book Blog

## Books by Stingray23

### **A Few Good Men**

Target Lizzy

Target Nina

Target Logan

Target Marie

Target Bella

# Contents

| | |
|---|---|
| Foreword | ix |
| The Navy Seal Creed | xi |
| | |
| Prologue | 1 |
| Chapter 1 | 7 |
| Chapter 2 | 13 |
| Chapter 3 | 23 |
| Chapter 4 | 35 |
| Chapter 5 | 43 |
| Chapter 6 | 51 |
| Chapter 7 | 59 |
| Chapter 8 | 67 |
| Chapter 9 | 75 |
| Chapter 10 | 83 |
| Chapter 11 | 91 |
| Chapter 12 | 99 |
| Chapter 13 | 105 |
| Chapter 14 | 113 |
| Chapter 15 | 121 |
| Chapter 16 | 129 |
| Chapter 17 | 137 |
| Chapter 18 | 145 |
| Chapter 19 | 151 |
| Chapter 20 | 161 |
| Epilogue | 167 |

| | |
|---|---|
| Jessika Klide writing as Stingray23 | 191 |
| Read Jessika Klide's newest, sexiest, and most talked about bestsellers... | 193 |
| Jessika Klide writing as Cindee Bartholomew | 197 |
| Jessika Klide writing as STINGRAY23 | 199 |
| Jessika Klide | 201 |
| JessikaKlide.com | 203 |

Human Trafficking happens everywhere. To Men, Women, and Children of All Ages, Races, Nationalities, and Genders.

If you or someone you know is a victim of human trafficking, reach out for help or report a tip now.

National Human Trafficking Hotline
**1-888-373-7888**

Text **"BEFREE"** or **"HELP"** to 233733

Email: help@humantraffickinghotline.org

National Center for Missing or Exploited Children
**1-800-THE-LOST**

# The Navy Seal Creed

In times of war or uncertainty there is a special breed of warrior ready to answer our Nation's call. A common man with uncommon desire to succeed.

Forged by adversity, he stands alongside America's finest special operations forces to serve his country, the American people, and protect their way of life.

I am that man.

My Trident is a symbol of honor and heritage. Bestowed upon me by the heroes that have gone before, it embodies the trust of those I have sworn to protect. By wearing the Trident, I accept the responsibility of my chosen profession and way of life. It is a privilege that I must earn every day.

My loyalty to Country and Team is

beyond reproach. I humbly serve as a guardian to my fellow Americans always ready to defend those who are unable to defend themselves. I do not advertise the nature of my work, nor seek recognition for my actions. I voluntarily accept the inherent hazards of my profession, placing the welfare and security of others before my own.

I serve with honor on and off the battlefield. The ability to control my emotions and my actions, regardless of circumstance, sets me apart from other men.

Uncompromising integrity is my standard. My character and honor are steadfast. My word is my bond.

We expect to lead and be led. In the absence of orders, I will take charge, lead my teammates, and accomplish the mission. I lead by example in all situations.

I will never quit. I persevere and thrive on adversity. My Nation expects me to be physically harder and mentally stronger than my enemies. If knocked down, I will get back up, every time. I will draw on every remaining ounce of strength to protect my teammates and to accomplish our mission. I am never out of the fight.

We demand discipline. We expect innovation. The lives of my teammates and the success of our mission depend on me — my technical skill, tactical proficiency, and attention to detail. My training is never complete.

We train for war and fight to win. I stand ready to bring the full spectrum of combat power to bear in order to achieve my mission and the goals established by my country. The execution of my duties will be swift and violent when required yet guided by the very principles that I serve to defend.

Brave men have fought and died building the proud tradition and feared reputation that I am bound to uphold. In the worst of conditions, the legacy of my teammates steadies my resolve and silently guides my every deed.

I will not fail.

# Target Marie

Marie Daniels isn't prepared for the tragedy of losing her best friends in a car crash. But digging deep, she finds the strength to take the Virgin Islands vacation they had planned together alone to mourn and honor them.

But a shocking chain of events rocks her world further when she comes face to face with the harsh reality of human trafficking after a pirate crew boards the yacht and takes her prisoner.

Forced to go along to survive, she finds herself falling in love with the beautiful barbarian (former Navy SEAL, now turned undercover agent for the DEA, Gabriel Managus) that claimed her as a spoil of war.

Will they make it out of the mission alive?

*To the victor belongs the spoils.*

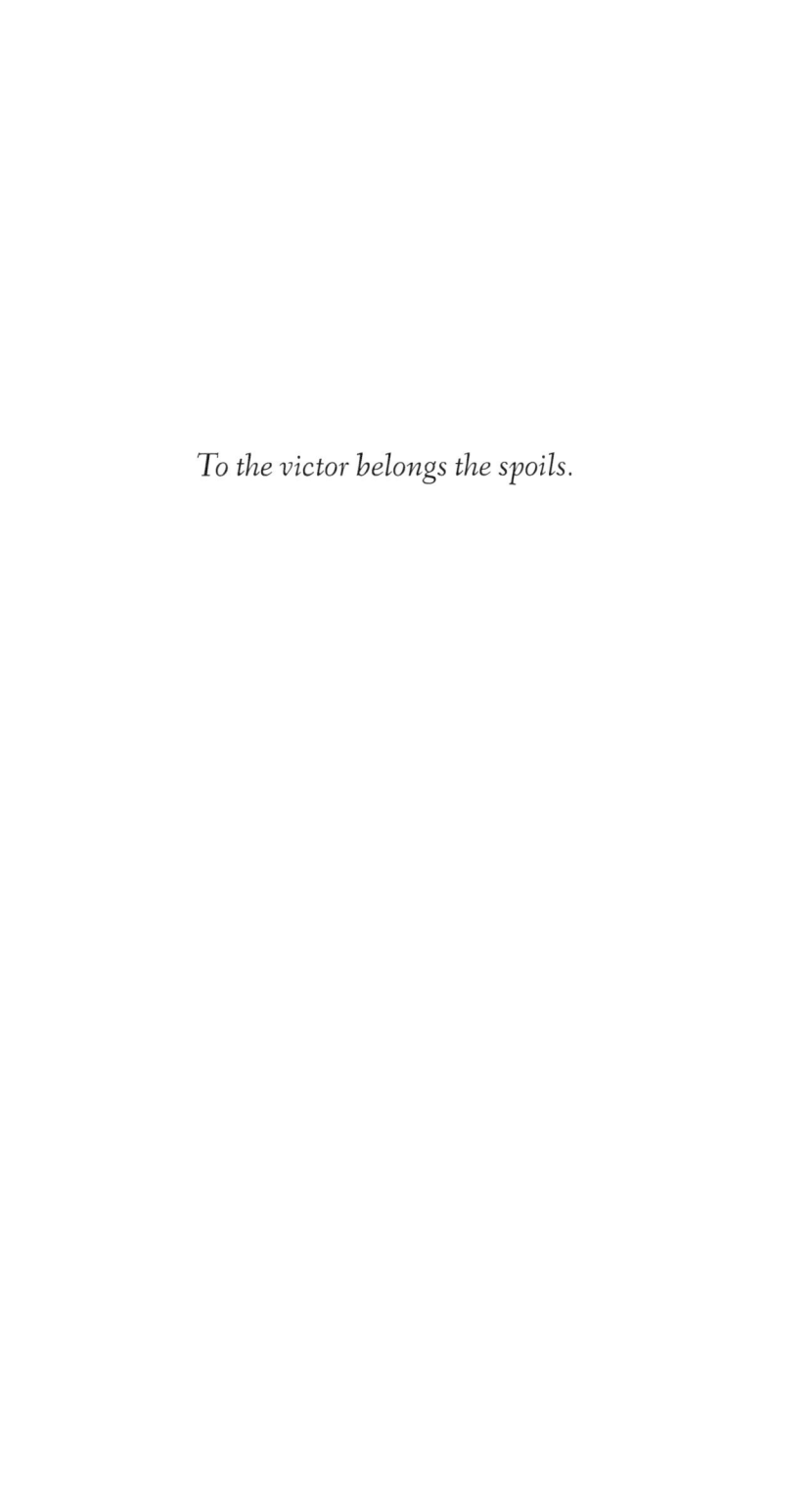

# Target Marie

# Prologue

*Marie*

"Come with us! Please?" Brenda tries her best to convince me while Karen dances and beckons, waving her hands.

"Go. Have a good time! I'll be fine. I have to finish this paper by midnight, or I'm going to flunk the class." I assure my best friends that I'm sitting this one out only because I have to, not because I want to.

"Okay then. We're going without you, but

we're going to bombard your phone with pics of us having the time of our lives!"

I laugh. "Then I'm turning it off because I won't get a damn thing done living vicariously through my phone."

They laugh as they dance out the door together. Karen asks Brenda, "What does that even mean?"

Brenda laughs as she throws her arm over Karen's shoulder and says, "Come on. Let's go."

I walk to the doorway to watch them get into the car and throw one more parting comment to them. "Be safe!"

They back out of the driveway, and I wave until they are out of sight.

Walking back inside, I turn my phone off. If I don't, I won't get this paper finished before midnight.

Walking into the kitchen, I grab a Red Bull from the refrigerator, pop the top, chug a few mouthfuls, then carry it back upstairs to my room.

This is all going to be worth it. I remind myself. You have to sacrifice to have more. Brenda and Karen are going to be teachers, while I'm going to be an airline pilot. They will marry men, settle down, and raise children content with living their lives with one man, possibly two, maybe three, in one place. While I will fly around the world, raking in four times the amount of money, enjoying different cultures and as many men as I want.

Settling in at my desk, I open my laptop to begin, but before I do, I let my imagination embrace the screen saver and visualize running into the aqua-colored waves from the sandy beach with the palm trees in the Virgin Islands. The three of us have planned a month-long yachting vacation to celebrate the conclusion of this phase of our lives.

I take a deep breath and imagine the smell of the salt air. "In one month, I will be swimming in those waters. Now, get to work."

---

## Gabriel

---

"There's a party tonight," I tell Pete, my DEA handler, as I throw back a shot of whiskey and scan the girls clad in skimpy bikinis playing volleyball on the beach.

"Did you get an invitation?" He asks as he lifts his beer to block his lips and watches the girls too.

"Yeah, I'm in. I'm actually the star performer tonight." I confirm as I stand, leave my money on the bar, and turn to go. "Tuesday at eight?"

"I'll be here." He drinks the brew without looking at me.

As I walk down the street on St. Thomas Island, I plan for the mission tonight. I've been undercover as Alejandro Barbados for five months now, working my way up the ranks of the King's Crew. My initial assignment was to learn about the drug trade, but I sniffed out a more significant issue, and the top brass in DC gave me the green light to shift gears. Running drugs is a much smaller piece of the King's Crew pie. They are pirating in human trafficking.

Tonight's raid is to snatch and grab some girls from a superyacht anchored offshore. This is my third boarding party.

So far, I've been able to avoid killing anyone. There are a hundred and one ways to fuck a person up and incapacitate them without taking their life. But if I have to snuff someone for mission success, I'm sanctioned to do so.

This has been the most challenging assignment

I have ever been on, including my Navy SEAL tours. Not physically, but emotionally. Going deep undercover means becoming the kind of person you are hunting, committing the crimes of the hunted. Thus, the more heinous the crime, the harder it is to handle, and this assignment is especially heinous because the victims are human beings. Young women my age or younger are treated worse than animals. They are drugged, tortured, humiliated, branded, and gang raped all before being enslaved to a life that offers no hope of freedom ever again. It is incomprehensible to the average person the degree to which these innocent girls suffer. Their lives are snatched from them and shattered forever.

In the DEA briefing, I learned that our agency has attempted to infiltrate this crew of pirates three times before, but those agents failed. Two were killed in the line of duty, and one withdrew. I was approached because I'm a former Navy SEAL and Special Warfare Operators are a breed above. Our training gives us an edge. With SEALs, failure is not an option, and neither is freedom. I said yes without hesitation.

# One

*One month later*
*2 AM*
*US Virgin Islands*

———

Gabriel

———

Standing on the beach, looking out at the yacht bathed in soft blue LED lights of tonight's target, I strip down to my speedo.

"Alejandro, are you sure?" Roberto asks me as

he picks my clothes up and tucks them under his arm.

"Yeah, man. I got this." I strap my knife to my thigh, then sling the plastic bag with the grappling hook launcher and rope over my shoulder. "Just give me twenty minutes before you crank the outboard."

"Twenty. Good luck."

"I don't need luck, compadre."

He salutes me. "Barbados, the Brutal Barbarian."

I smirk, shaking my head. "Twenty, Roberto. Not nineteen." Then I wade out into the water and dive into the darkness.

Enjoying the solitude of submersion, I swim under the surface until my breath is gone. Then I slowly break the plane between water and air, inhale a massive lung-bursting breath, then slip down out of sight, repeating the sequence until I'm treading water next to the yacht.

When we met up for tonight's raid, the buzz this afternoon was that an entire crew was taken down last night. If that is true, then there will be a shift in the organization's structure and an opportunity for me to advance higher up their chain of command.

I'm growing impatient with the length of time it's taking me to discover where the girls are being taken to be sold, so I crippled the trolling motor we use on the dinghy. Roberto wanted to call off the raid, but I insisted we proceed, ensuring my name is circulated among the pirates.

Typically, our crew of six to ten men takes the dinghy to the vessel and board as an overwhelming force, but I will board the yacht alone to disable the vessel's radios, taking out any crew members along the way.

Once the pirates are on board, they will drug everyone, then extract those they can sell. Once we are back at the hideout, the victims are isolated and kept until being sold into the human sex trafficking business. The less compliant, the more drugs are used to control them. The faster they adapt, the better their chance of survival.

I remove the grappling gun, then launch the steel hook covered with fabric over the railing. The soft thud and the slack in the line confirm it has landed. I pull the rope tight, and it grabs the railing. Returning the launcher to the bag, I seal it with air to keep it afloat, then set it free. The crew will retrieve it when they arrive.

The clouds slide over the moon, and darkness descends.

Time to get to work. I hoist myself up the rope.

---

*Meanwhile, onboard the yacht ...*

---

*Marie*

---

Ugh! Another sleepless night.

I sigh, giving up the effort to drift into dreamland, staring up at the cabin ceiling as the nagging weight of depression that refuses to go away settles on my chest and pools in my eyes.

Losing my best friends in a car accident has jarred me to my core, and two months later, I'm still dealing daily with the emotional fallout.

I had hoped that going ahead with our plans to sail around the Virgin Islands, carrying on for Brenda and Karen, living my best life to honor their memory, would help clear away this nagging depression. But, so far, the peaceful silence has only amplified my loss.

I sit on the bed and grab a ponytail tie. Twisting my long hair up into a loose who-cares-if-half-is-sprouting-out-in-all-directions bun, I take a deep breath, then stretch, owning my insomnia. Then I slip into my bikini and head out of the cabin for some fresh air and moonlight.

Walking out onto the deck, I stop and inhale a deep, cleansing breath of the salty air. Then stroll to the handrail and peer down at the black water. The small waves, too insignificant to rock the yacht, softly slap against the side.

The sight lulls my tired mind into a peaceful trance-like state. But the clouds covering the moonlight slide away. Lifting my face to look out over the vast body of water, I enjoy the moonlight dancing on the surface of the water as the tears of loss slip down my cheeks.

I should have realized it was too soon to be alone and flown to San Diego to hang out with my stepbrother instead. Cash wouldn't have minded. He is always down for spending time with me, and he gives the best hugs.

I sigh and wipe away the tears. His "Be brave,

beautiful" always makes me feel like I can handle anything.

I'll call him when we go ashore again. Hopefully, hearing his voice will help clear out this clusterfuck of emotion doing a number on my psyche.

I stare up at the sky. Without the interference of ground lights, the billions of twinkling stars are beautiful.

# Two

Gabriel

———

Peering over the edge of the deck, I survey the scene.

Dammit. What is she doing on deck?

I glance at my G-shock watch. It's been fourteen minutes. The crew will crank the outboard in six minutes. I have one minute to decide how to handle this.

She's resting on the rail with her face lifted to the sky. Her hair is in a messy bun on top of her head. Her curvy body silhouetted against the moonlight. This girl will bring top dollar to the pirates.

Be gentle. Try not to bruise her.

I pull myself on board slowly to avoid detection, watching her, being careful to maintain the element of surprise.

She lifts her hand to her face and wipes away tears. Dammit, she's emotional. Better make this quick. I jump over the rail. Landing in a crouch like a cat on the deck with only a slight thud to announce my arrival, but she stiffens, startled.

As she spins around to face me, I hurl myself toward her, coming in hot. Her eyes flare as her mouth falls open, and she fills her lungs to scream.

What the fucking hell? Marie Daniels? The drop-dead gorgeous little sister of Cash Cohen, my BUD/S training officer? Cash threatened every last one of us to keep our distance from her. She was off-limits. Not only because she was his little sister, but because she was underage, "Jailbait." Then he lectured on the dangers of Frog hogs, SEAL whores.

What the fucking hell is Marie doing on a yacht in the Virgin Islands? And what the fucking hell am I going to do?

As I advance, I unsheathe my knife, flipping it

over, blade down, so it lays harmlessly against her throat.

The first order of business is to keep her from screaming. After that, it depends on whether or not she recognizes me.

---

*Marie*

---

*Holy Hell! Where did you come from?*

My mind screams while my throat chokes on the words.

Watching the majestic mass of man rush across the deck to me, I brace against the railing. Scared shitless, my mind absorbs every detail of the approaching threat. He's very tall with swole, ripped, shredded muscles. His face is 'swoony' handsome with black hair, big dark brows, light-colored eyes, a straight nose, and full sculpted lips framed by an unshaven scruff.

He's absolutely gorgeous! A perfect physical specimen of manliness.

*Knife!*

I raise my hands to shield myself, but it is useless. They land without any effect except to absorb the initial jolt of electricity from his body. Then his speedo presses into my hips, pinning me in place, and he clamps one hand over my mouth while the other holds the cold steel of the knife blade against my jugular.

As every fiber of my threatened body amps up to supercharged sensitivity from the spike of adrenaline, waves of confusing feelings wash over me.

Am I about to join Brenda and Karen? The thought scares the hell out of me. I close my eyes, holding my breath, afraid the wild pounding of my heart will cause my neck to be sliced.

My hands and hips tingle from his touch like an electric current, churning up my insides, stirring my.... Dear God, he smells heavenly, a sensual scent of sea and musk. Overwhelmed, I turn my face away. His hot breath blows across my vulnerable neck caressingly as he studies my face.

Trapped, I wait for him to do something, to say something, but he simply holds his position, causing wave after wave of ... what the fuck is wrong with me ... desire to crash through my fear.

His masculinity is undeniable. Testosterone reeks from his pores. Is he going to rape me? The thought makes me weak.

Finally, a low, deep rumble from his chest commands, "Look at me."

I obey, lifting my eyes to his, and ... holy hell .... I stare into the most amazing, amber-colored eyes, boring into mine, piercing my heart and seizing my soul.

My knees buckle....

"Christ," he swears as I swoon.

...

I open my eyes to see the beautiful barbarian's face hovering inches over mine. A few wet tresses dangle free. His strong jaw is covered in a thick, rough scruff. He hasn't shaved in days.

He whispers, "You're okay," and I look at his mouth. His rough dark scruff surrounds full, luscious lips, and my mouth waters when they whisper, "Don't make a sound."

I look into his amazing amber eyes, outlined with thick, long, black lashes framed by a hawkish gaze, searching mine. There is no malice in them. There is only deep concern.

I'm wrapped in his strong arms lying on the

deck under a billion stars, and I wonder if I'm dreaming.

He whispers, "I'm going to pick you up and carry you inside."

I nod, and he stands, holding my hand. Watching his magnificent body uncoil as he lifts me to my feet is a sight I will never forget. He bends down, puts me over his shoulder, and runs with me to the stairs, then into the helm.

He drops me in the captain's chair and whispers his command with a deadly tone, "Don't break silence and don't fucking move." His voice is harsh, cutting, cold, and I stare stunned as he violently stabs the console with his knife. Disabling the radios and crippling the yacht's ability to communicate that it's under attack. The force of each thrust sends uncontrollable shivers through me.

He glances out over the deck, and I follow his gaze. There are two male silhouettes leaning over the railing.

Holy Fuck! He isn't alone! I have to get away!

I jump out of the chair, terrorized, and turn to flee. Of course, he isn't alone!

But before I reach the doorway, his hand grabs my hair and snatches my body back against his.

The pain kills the panic instantly but only heightens the rush of desire that hits me when my body crashes against his.

He leans down, and his dominance over me with his breath caressing the sensitive spot just under my earlobe sends heightened sensations of desire straight down there.

Dammit! My tits draw up taut and tight, and he sees how turned on I am.

His deep tone vibrates my eardrum as he softly speaks directly into my ear, "Where are the captain's quarters?"

Dear lord, goosebumps break out all over. That shouldn't sound so sexy, but it does. My mouth goes dry, and I can't answer him, so I lift my arm and point the way.

He drags me by my hair down the hall to the captain's quarters, then stops and pulls my face up to his.

Holy! Fuck! His eyes have changed! A warrior looks at me. Fierce, ferocious, and ready to fight. I tremble, truly terrified now. Not for myself. He has no intentions of killing me, or I would be dead, but for anyone who stands in his way. Killing is not an issue for him.

His breath blows hard against my face, stirring

the tiny white hairs making me feel more alive than I have ever felt in my life, and as I search his eyes, I realize that the only way to survive is with him. For some reason, he has chosen me.

His amber eyes spit fire into mine as he whispers, "Stay on my six. I move. You move. You copy?"

I nod, inhaling a calming lung full of his sweet breath deep down inside, and I realize I want more with this man.

He releases me, then pushes the door open, flips the light on, and walks straight at the captain, who is standing in the doorway of his bathroom with a pistol pointed at my pirate's chest.

OH. MY. GOD! I start to shake.

A low rumble emits from my man, and the captain threatens him. "I'll kill you!" But the pistol is shaking wildly, and I register why I was told to stay on my pirate's six and move when he moved. His body will block the bullet.

He growls, "You better get after it then, motherfucker."

But the captain is too terrified to do it, and in six steps, my badass pirate snatches the weapon out of his hands. Then in one powerful movement, the pirate rears all the way back and swings with all six-foot-four-or-more, two-hundred-thirty-pounds-give-or-take and knocks said motherfucker over like a downed tree. He was hit so hard his dead weight literally bounces off the floor.

# Three

Gabriel

———

I grab Marie's wrist, intending to drag her with me back up to the deck. She didn't recognize me, and if we can reach the upper deck before the others see her, I will have another opportunity to save her. If she hadn't fainted, she would already be free, but she did.

I step around her and pull her arm, but she's frozen to the spot, staring at the captain.

"Is he dead?" She whispers.

"Negative. Unconscious." I pull gently again. "Come on."

But she doesn't move. Instead, she looks at me with an expression of wonder on her face. I've seen the look many times before. She's in shock.

"We're running out of time." I bend over and hoist her onto my shoulder again, then sprint up to the deck with her. I head straight to the opposite side from the dinghy. At the railing, I set her down as tell her, "Swim to the moon for as long as you can, then float. The tide will wash you ashore."

She stares at me, stunned. "You're letting me go?"

"Yes," I sigh. Why do girls talk so much? I take a step toward her, preparing to pick her up and throw her ass overboard myself. Then the sounds of scuffling and screams reach us, and she turns to look that way. I jerk her arm, and she looks back at me. The expression on her beautiful face is not terror but awe.

I don't know what the hell she's thinking, but she isn't moving fast enough.

"GO!"

---

*Marie*

The screams from the girls explode the conflicting emotions inside me. Both panic and passion clash as I look at the man choosing to save me.

I stare up at his handsome face, burning into my mind his wild, angry, desperate expression, and time stands still as it hits me. He is a good man in a bad situation.

Questions streak across my mind in the frozen moment.

How does a good man lose his way?

How does a good man go wrong?

I think about my brother and this man's warrior face. He spoke military lingo. 'Stay on my six,' and 'copy that.'

Is he suffering from post-traumatic stress disorder?

If Cash became lost in his own mind ... if his demons haunted him, would someone save him if they could?

Can I help this man?

Then I realize I already have. That's why he's letting me go.

But why would he join a pirate crew?

He takes a threatening step toward me and breaks the spell.

I don't want to ever forget him. He's set me free from the survivor's guilt I was wallowing in, and now this nightmare situation. Only a genuinely honorable man would break his gang ties and risk his own life.

I launch myself on him, throwing my arms around his neck, and planting my lips on his. For a brief moment, he returns my kiss, and my god, he tastes like heaven!

Then he stiffens, grabs my bun again, and pulls me off. He opens his mouth and shouts for me to "GO, dammit, before it's too late."

I whisper, "Thank you. I will never forget you." Then I scramble over the railing to dive off.

———

Gabriel

———

Roberto yells behind me. "Bro, you need some help with that one?"

The look on Marie's face is sheer terror, and I cringe at the sound of his voice. "Negative. She's not going anywhere." I shout over my shoulder as I latch onto Marie's bun, halting her escape.

Pushing all kindness and compassion out of my mind, locking it away as SEALs are trained to do, there isn't anything I can do now but become the brutal barbarian to save us both. She fucked around, stole a kiss, and now, she's fucked herself out of her freedom. She should have just fucking jumped!

Roberto laughs as he approaches, enjoying the way I drag her by her hair back over the railing. "Control the head, and the body will follow," I tell him.

I know my grip is hurting her, but she has to realize the danger she has put us both in. Her hands claw at mine, trying to ease the pain, as tears spill down her cheeks and a whimper slips out of her mouth. The door I slammed, bangs, wanting to open.

Fuck me! I lift her off her feet until her toes are dangling, intending to brutally make her submit by kissing the ever-loving fuck out of her mouth. My other hand grips her throat and squeezes. But I'm careful not to cause her to lose consciousness. I press just enough to bruise her. Knowing the marks I leave will ensure she isn't sold until they heal. Buying time to sort out what to do.

But as soon as I kiss her, she willingly submits, and I lose myself in her softness and the sweetness of her taste. She parts her teeth, inviting me in, and when her tongue touches mine, my cock gets rock hard, growing in my speedo.

I hear Roberto chuckling as he walks away to give directions to the men bringing the drugged, unconscious bodies of the women we are stealing on deck.

My thumb strokes the soft skin of Marie's neck, and I feel the vibration as a soft moan in her throat. Her hands now gently hold on to mine, asking me to cherish her. The more I kiss her, the more I want her. Thrusting my tongue down her throat over and over again. Claiming her, I grab her ass, crushing her wanton body against mine.

A ravenous moan fills the air, and I'm not sure if it's mine or hers.

"Yo, Alejandro. Let's go. We got what we want." Roberto calls out, and I break the kiss. Lifting my face from hers, I wait to answer him, enjoying the submissive look in Marie's eyes as she accepts her fate.

---

*Marie*

---

Jesus, I'm like putty right now. I touch my lips, staring into those fantastic amber eyes. That kiss was everything!

"Stay on my six. I move. You move. You copy?"

I nod, and Alejandro gives me a killer wink that rocks my world all over again, then he takes my wrist and leads me to the other side of the yacht.

I scan the scene, and the horror of human trafficking shakes me. About ten girls are lying unconscious on the deck. Two pirates are tying their hands and feet together, while two more pick them up, carry them to the side, and hoist them overboard.

Alejandro announces, "I'm keeping this one for myself."

Roberto laughs and tosses him a bundle of

clothes. He drops my wrist to catch them, then pops the fabric to release the knot, and a pair of white sneakers, jeans, and a muscle tank top fall to the ground. He unstraps his knife sheath and drops it on top as he bends over and grabs the jeans. When he lifts his foot to step into them, he nearly loses his balance, and I reach out to steady him.

Roberto laughs again, then turns back to help the others.

As he pulls the jeans up over his speedo, I marvel at how I could have missed that massive muscle between his legs. He's definitely endowed in that department too. He has to bend forward slightly to tuck it into his pants before he can zip up and button the jeans. While he maneuvers it into position, I bend down and retrieve the white muscle tank top for him. I hold it out for him to take when he's ready, and he gives me a little smirk when he pulls it out of my hands. Then slips it over his head and pushes his huge arms through the oversized holes. As he pulls the hem down and tucks it in his jeans, I wonder how he fits his broad frame into a regular cut shirt.

Next, I kneel down and offer to help him with his shoes. He slips each foot inside, and I pull the backs over his heel. Then I pick up the knife in its sheath and hand it to him.

For the first time, he smiles, and I see how truly handsome he is. His teeth are white and straight. He takes it from me and straps it around his leg, then he tests the angle by pulling it out, then sticking it back in.

Satisfied, he reaches into a pocket, pulls out a white bandana dotted with a dark logo, and as he ties it around his head, effectively controlling his long hair, he stares at me.

I admire the change. He looks more like a pirate businessman than a barbarian now. I smirk and nod at his transformation, and he gives me that killer wink again.

Then he's reaching into another pants pocket and pulls out a black dog tag from a different pocket. The insignia is a king's crown with his name stenciled on it. He opens the chain and offers it. I step forward and bow my head, and he slips it over, then he lifts my face by gently pulling my chin up, and I stare into those amazing amber eyes again. The desire I see in his assures me that I am claimed and therefore protected.

Then he stands, folding his arms over his chest, with his hips cocked forward, and leans back, turning into a badass right before my eyes. The man looks like he eats weaklings for breakfast.

He observes the crew of pirates as they lower the women one by one over the side. I step closer to him, so his broad back blocks my view, and I can feel his strength oozing off his body. I know I'm going to need it.

When it's my turn, Alejandro faces me, opens his arms, and says, "Jump on."

I do as I'm told. Placing my hands on his shoulders, I jump, and he grabs my ass, pulling me tight against him. I wrap my legs around his waist, hook my hands around his neck, and ride him as he steps over the railing, then scales down the rope to a dinghy waiting below. His strength and agility make it seem effortless.

As his massive muscles move under me, the scent of his musk fills my nostrils, and I marvel at how safe he makes me feel. Then the thought of why he shouldn't have to makes me more determined than ever to be compliant.

This man is a total badass, and by God, I'm going to prove myself worthy of him.

As he sets me down in the boat, I turn my face away from his protection to see the bodies of the other women stacked on top of each other like potatoes in a bin, and I wonder if the ones on the bottom will survive the crushing dead weight from the ones on top.

I look up at him and thank my stars, this good man wants me.

# Four

Gabriel

———

Marie understands the horror she faces now and understands what her role is. Keeping her eyes locked on my face, she waits for my instructions. I look down where I want her to sit, and she sinks slowly until her ass hits bottom. Never breaking eye contact.

Before I sit down with her, I look over the faces of my crew staring at us, and I make sure they understand that if I fight to keep her, they will die. Then I sit, folding my body around her, and cradle her against my chest as the boat begins the long journey back.

She snuggles up, resting her head on my chest, and before long, I realize she's fallen asleep.

Good. She needs to be alert and ready to fight if it comes to that. I'm not at all sure how claiming her before the higher-ranking members of the pirate crew have looked her over will go down. They have a structured chain of command, but it isn't firm. It's okay in most instances to break the rules, but if you're challenged for coloring outside the lines, you have to fight or back down, and backing down has never been an option for me.

Sitting here holding this angel as we plow through the ocean heading to a hidden pirate cove in a dinghy full of enemy combatants with victims of human trafficking as cargo is a surreal moment.

I lay my head on my arm, pretending to rest as well. But instead, I stare at her, enjoying her presence. My heart was as hard and cold as it has ever been before. I didn't realize how close I had come to losing my soul to this mission. I hate with every fiber of my being that she is here, she should be free, but I can't deny, I'm glad to have her company. She's indirectly a part of my SEAL family, and her connection to my past is strangely grounding.

Before, my ego would have been bruised that she didn't recognize me, but now, I'm just thankful she will behave genuinely. Which will make keeping her safe while maintaining my cover and continuing the mission possible.

I reach out and tuck a stray strand of hair that's fallen out of her messy bun behind her ear. She's petite, not weighing 120 pounds, but she isn't fragile. She's muscular and strong. She hasn't broken down during all this, even after her adrenaline dump. She isn't a blubbering crybaby or a whining bitch who would make this difficult situation a nightmare. But then again, she's Cash's little sister. Of course, she's tough as nails.

The dinghy begins a slow right turn heading into the hidden cove, and her body weight shifts. I tighten my hold to stabilize her, and she stirs, lifting her head.

As she looks around, the wildness in her eyes creates a bottleneck in my throat as my breath and blood are trapped by its constriction. If she freaks now, all hell will break loose when we get inside with the rest of the crew. They will try to take her away from me, and I won't be able to stop them.

Their overwhelming numbers will win. But if she remains submissive and obedient to my command, then I can fight for her if any one of them challenges me to take her for themselves.

Although, I have my own hand-picked band of loyalists within the pirate crew. They do not function like SEAL teams. They don't operate as a single unit for the greater good. They work as a band of individuals with a common goal.

"Hey," I whisper. "Look at me."

———

*Marie*

———

Oh my god. I wasn't dreaming. This is really happening! I fight for control over my terror.

I latch onto Alejandro's calm eyes and swallow the fear that threatens to destroy everything.

He whispers. "You're okay. I got you. Breathe deep. In ... and ... out."

His soft expression reassures me, and I press my trembling lips together. Then I inhale and exhale with him, and the terror recedes.

He smirks as he removes my hair bow and my long tresses catch the wind, whipping around us, then his deep voice softly says, "Good girl."

I don't know why that sends a thrill through me, but it does. I lean toward him, closing my eyes, offering him my lips, wanting to lose myself in him and not think about what's about to happen.

A throaty moan emits from him as his hand wraps itself in my hair and jerks my head back. His eyes flash fiercely into mine, warning me, and the thought that I can't initiate physical contact between us is planted firmly in my mind as painful tears form.

But he leans forward to give me what I asked for. Just before our lips touch, he whispers, "Do precisely what I tell you to do and nothing more."

I inhale the sweetness of his breath. Close my eyes with the softness of his lips. Melt into a willing submissive with the command of his mouth. I'm filled with not only a desire to serve him but a need to hear, 'Good girl' again.

As I lose myself to his control, I internalize the choice I've made. I must be obedient to him. I can trust his military training to protect me.

———

# Gabriel

---

God, this woman is rocking my world. Her tongue teases mine, and it's like my first fucking kiss. Fireworks.

As we approach the cove, the dinghy decreases speed, and I release her mouth. Needing to communicate what's about to happen with her so she's prepared and doesn't freak the fuck out. She's intelligent and understands what she's up against, but she isn't prepared for what's about to go down. No one is. But she has to endure it with me, or she runs the risk of being taken from me.

Hovering my lips over hers, I whisper her instructions. "You must trust me. Whatever happens once we get inside, whatever you see, whatever you feel or think, you must trust me and do precisely what I tell you to do. Nothing more. Nothing less."

Her beautiful eyes are big saucers, and I see the fear in them. "These men are barbarians. If I'm challenged for you ... and, babe, you're beautiful, so it's a serious probability ... I won't back down, and I won't give you up. Do you understand?"

She nods, frowning, then asks, "Why are you doing this?"

I narrow my eyes and decide to tell her as much truth as I can. Knowing it will ground her and give her the strength she needs to follow my lead without question, and hopefully, stave off some of the shock at what she will see. "For Cash."

She blinks a few times, absorbing my words, then she frowns again. I reach up and put that stray strand of her hair behind her ear once more. "Your brother, not money."

Tears well up in her eyes, and she nods, then bites her lip and swallows the lump in her throat. "Are you a former SEAL then?"

"Yes."

"What happened?" Her eyes search mine, and I can't believe she's staring at me, concerned for my well-being in the midst of what's happening around us.

"I'll explain later."

She nods. "I'll do precisely what you tell me to do. Nothing more. Nothing less. I will stick to your six and move when you move. I will be submissive and suck your cock in front of the whole damn group if that's what you command me to do."

I chuckle at that. "That's not a bad idea."

# Five

*Marie*

———

Alejandro sits up to watch our approach to shore, and I glance in that direction. From the looks of it, we are running right up to a sheer cliff of giant boulders. The men in the dinghy kneel, holding onto the sides. Before we ram the rocks, the motor shuts off, and we coast right up to them.

The thought that they have done this many times sends shivers through me. I wonder how many women they have taken.

The pirates bailout, holding on to the boat's sides, and wade through the water straight at the boulders. The sun is just starting to break the horizon, and there is enough light to see a small gap in the water between two rocks.

Alejandro puts his hand on top of my head and pushes it down, but not before seeing the men submerge and realize they are swimming the dinghy through the gap. Then darkness envelops us as the rocks block out the sun, and I reach out to touch Alejandro. He places his hand over mine and gives me a gentle, reassuring squeeze.

When we emerge from the darkness, we are in a small lagoon. I look around, marveling at the beauty. Then I look into Alejandro's face. He is frowning at me. Instantly, I avert my eyes and look down. He tips my face to his and puts two fingers to his eyes. I nod, and he stands in the boat.

I keep my eyes on my man, resisting the urge to look around, and focus my attention instead on the noises. Legs splash in the water as the crew walks the dinghy to shore. The sound of ATVs approaching rumbles louder and louder. Then the boat is being dragged onto land, and Alejandro jumps out.

The ATVs arrive and idle. I wait, not wanting to look around but unsure if I should have followed

Alejandro or not. I can hear men talking but can't make out their words.

Then my pirate appears, reaching over the side for me. I stand up and walk to him. Keeping my eyes focused on his face, I lean over as his hands slide around my waist, and I place my hands on his shoulders. He lifts me out like I weigh nothing, allows my body to slide down his, and I'm thankful for the grounding contact. Then he removes his bandana, rolls it into a blindfold, and ties it over my eyes.

Next, he picks me up and carries me to an ATV. He sets me on the seat, then swings his leg over and scoots his groin uptight. My legs rest across his thigh, and when he reaches for the handlebars, my arm slips around his waist to hang on. He whispers, "Good girl." And I melt.

Then he cranks it, puts it in gear, and eases off. As we travel, I hug him tight, resting my head on his chest, enjoying the closeness of his essence. I don't know what lies ahead, but I'm content right now to live in the moment.

---

## Gabriel

Traveling with Marie snuggled up is the best feeling in the world, and I allow myself the freedom to enjoy her in this brief respite. She is a gorgeous girl physically, but I find myself even more drawn to her character. She should be frightened, or at the least, anxious, but instead, she's trusting. She's smart, and that's a massive turn-on to me. If the circumstances were normal, I would chase her relentlessly until she surrendered her booty to me.

At the end of the cave tunnel, I stop the ATV, park it along the inner wall with the others, turn it off, and dismount. Then I help Marie off and inform her, "We'll walk the rest of the way."

She holds her hand out for mine, and I thread my fingers through hers, bonding us together and lead her away. The ground is soft and sandy, so the going is slow.

She asks, "Are we alone? I don't hear anyone else."

"Affirmative."

"May I ask you how you know Cash?"

"He was my training officer during BUD/S."

"Oh." She answers, then walks along silently

for less than a minute. "Did you pass or wash out?"

I chuckle. It's a legit question. Roughly 70% don't make it through. "I passed."

She stumbles and grabs my arm with her other hand, causing her tits to press into it, which causes a surge in blood to flow below. Damn. I'm going to walk in and challenge the Board with a hard-on. Well, at least the reason I'm willing to fight to keep her will be evident.

She continues walking, holding on, and it begins to feel more like a stroll with my girl than a kidnapping victim forced to comply with my wishes.

"How old are you?"

I shake my head. Girls! They are always talking. I can't imagine living in their headspace. "Twenty-eight. You?"

"Twenty-three." She adds, "I'm here alone because I lost my best friends in a car accident a few months ago. We had scheduled this trip to celebrate our graduation. Our last hoorah together before we went our separate ways."

I squeeze her hand. That's why she was crying on deck.

"Before anything else happens," she stops and turns to face me. "I want to thank you for rescuing me from survivor's guilt. I was wallowing in when you showed up."

Watching her lips move, forming her words because her eyes are covered, sends another surge of blood flowing below. Damn. The thought of those lips wrapped around my cock and sucking my brain through my vein nearly drowns out the sweet words of gratitude she says. Then she adds, "Do you believe in destiny? I do."

I reach up, pinch her chin, then trace my thumb over perfect lips. The urge to kiss her again sends my hand to the nape of her neck, and I put our hands behind her back to pull her to me. She falls forward, landing on my chest, and her free hand slides around my waist.

"Mmm," my tongue thrusts slowly into her appreciative mouth. After the kiss, I tell her. "I'll let you thank me properly later if you still feel the same way."

She licks her lips and nods. "I'm going to be brave."

My heart feels the weight of her words, and I know she's going to do her best to pull this off and survive. My job is to keep her mental scarring from what's about to go down to a minimum. Regardless of what happens between us after this mission is over, she belongs to me now. I will protect her from the evil within the walls we are about to enter. I kiss her forehead, then begin walking toward the headquarters to be debriefed by the Board.

After a few seconds, she says, "My name is Marie Daniels, by the way."

"I know." I smile, and I feel her surprise in her hand when she pulls slightly against me. "Cash warned us not to fuck around with you. You were off-limits. 'Jailbait' is the exact word he used."

She laughs, and the sound is melodic, not cackling. "That was a long time ago, Alejandro." Then she hugs my arm up between her tits again. "Alejandro isn't your real name, is it?"

I don't respond, and she lets the question go unanswered.

"We're here," I tell her. "No more talking. Not even if you're asked a question. I am the only one you are to look at, respond to, answer, obey. Do you copy?"

"Copy that." She says, "I can do this. I will do this. I want to live, but more importantly, I want to live with you."

I remove the bandana from her eyes and stare into them as I wrap it around my head again. "Stay frosty."

# Six

*Meanwhile, at the Chicken Ranch. Coq Blockers, Inc. Headquarters in Las Vegas, NV ...*

---

Crockett

---

"Cash Cohen! What a surprise, brother!"

"Crockett, it's good to hear your voice, man."

"It's been too long. You need to come by Suds After BUD/S and let me buy you a beer."

"I will. But first, I need to ask you if the rumors

are true that you've put your team back together and are hunting human traffickers."

I missed the tension in his voice before, but clearly, he is stressed out over something. "That's affirmative. You need our services?"

"I'm afraid so. My little sister was on a yacht in the Virgin Islands, and she's missing."

"Missing or taken?"

"I'm sorry. I'm rattled. Taken. My dad just called and told me."

"Hang on." I snap my fingers, and both Nina and Meghan's eyes focus on me. "I'm going to have Nina record your call."

Nina rushes to the conference room where the media control console is, and when she comes back to stand in the doorway, I tell Cash. "Give me what you know so far."

"Not a whole hell of a lot."

"Every little bit helps."

"My dad said he got a call from the police in the Virgin Islands. My sister was vacationing on a yacht. About five hours ago, a crew of pirates boarded. They took the young females off. Marie was one of them."

"Was anyone killed?"

"He didn't say. He was pretty shaken up. I

could hear my stepmom wailing in the background. She's Marie's mom."

"Okay. I'm going to call our FBI contact and see what I can learn. I'll call you back."

"Rocket, count me in on the mission."

"No, man. That's not a good idea. She's family. Let us handle this."

"I'll go alone then."

I look at Nina, and she tilts her head and smirks. It was worth a try, but no one excepted him to agree to stand down. It's not what SEALs do, ever.

"Take the first flight out to Las Vegas. Text me when you know your arrival time. Someone will pick you up and bring you here. We won't leave without you."

"Copy that. Cohen, out."

Meghan calls Zane Lockhart. He answers on the first ring. "Ambassador, to what do I owe this honor?"

She rolls her eyes, despite the seriousness of her call. Meghan is single, and although Zane is happily married, he used to be a player and enjoys teasing her. "Zane, Meghan. You're on speaker."

"Ha. Thanks for the warning, babe."

She rolls her eyes again, and that's my cue to speak.

"Zane, Rocket. Just got a call from Cash Cohen. His little sister Marie has been snatched off a yacht in the Virgin Islands. We need you to find out all you can about what is happening down there. The team will fly out as soon as Cash arrives."

"Roger that. I'm on it." He hangs up.

Nina comes to stand by me. "I've sent the team a text alert. Wheels up in four. Tropical gear."

I nod. "Meghan, you up for a trip to the Virgin Islands?"

"Oh, abso-fucking-lutely. I'll go pack my gear." She smiles, then walks out.

Nina says, "Are you playing matchmaker too?"

I grin. "I'm just thinking of ways to keep Cash in the game without being in the game."

She punches my arm. "You're a sly dog, Crockett."

I chuckle.

An hour later, Dirk Sam, our pilot, checks in first. "Inbound with Franks, Black, and Andrews. Malone, Luce, and Cohen in two. Davis pickup in PCB, Florida at refuel."

Nina answers. "Roger that."

"Let's get to The Coop, Foxtrot. There are girls to save."

She follows me out the door and slides into the Gator ATV next to me. "You know, once in a while, I'd like to get to go out in the field too."

I cut my eyes at her. "Are you jealous Meghan's going?"

She nods, "Hell yeah, I am. The Virgin Islands? Come on!"

I laugh at her. "If you can pack all the shit you'll need in two hours, you can come too."

She grins, "You bet your ass I can." Then she throws her arms around me and tries to kiss me.

"HEY! You're going to make me wreck!" I lean away, but she manages to plant a wet kiss on my cheek. Then she sits down, grabs her phone, and starts a list of gear she'll need to pack. "I'm going to have to go shopping sometime while we're there. I'll need a swimsuit to blend it."

I grin, "Of course, you will."

Our S-70 Sikorsky helicopter buzzes overhead. When we arrive at The Coop, our operations station, the guys are already unloaded, and Dirk is pulling pitch to head back to Vegas.

We all walk in together, and usually, since Nina is our targeting officer, she greets everyone, then gives them a quick rundown before the actual mission briefing. But this time, she heads straight back to the warehouse to pack her gear.

Mike Franks, my number two, asks the obvious. "Where is she going?"

"To pack."

"She's going with us?" His eyebrows raise.

"I told her if you could pack everything she needs in two hours, then she could come too."

"And she thinks she can?" Jack Black, my number three, asks, laughing as he walks over to the door and peers in. "Oh, lord!" He chuckles hard and looks back at me. "That was a mistake, brother! She's a tornado right now, and the warehouse is her trailer park!"

Brody Andrews says, "Dibs on a window seat!"

Just then, Meghan walks through the door with her gear and sets it down. "Let's roll, boys!"

Franks rolls his eyes and looks at me like I've lost my fucking mind. "Really? The Ambassador is going too?"

I nod. "That's affirmative."

Jack shouts, "Dibs on a window seat!" And he and Brody high-five each other.

Meghan looks around, "Where's Nina?"

I shrug, "Do you honestly think I could tell her no when I told you yes?"

She squeals and runs through the door to the warehouse.

Franks says, "Explain yourself, one."

So, I tell them what little I know and why Meghan is going.

Frank agrees, "Good call, brother. I'm with you on that decision. She will make an excellent distraction for Cohen. But Nina?"

I shrug again and rephrase my previous answer. "There is no way in hell I could tell her no when it was my idea for Meghan to go. But I did stipulate she has to be packed and ready when the wheels are up. We aren't waiting on her."

Franks unzips his bag and looks inside. "So, how old is Cash's little sister now?"

"She's old enough to take a trip to the Virgin Islands without a chaperone."

"Fuck, man, we're getting old!"

# Seven

*Marie*

———

His command to 'stay frosty' is SEAL lingo for 'keep your shit together.' I nod and smirk at him, then give him a slight twitch of an eyewink, and he rolls his eyes.

"Marie, this is not a game. These men are powerful and evil. Violence is the way they maintain control. Blood is the way you win."

I nod and pray that Alejandro can keep me for himself.

"Head bowed. Eyes down. Don't look around. It'll be easier."

I lick my lips and remind him he is a SEAL. "The only easy day was yesterday."

He smiles, "Shush now."

Then the most beautiful man in the world turns away and walks across the parking lot to the building where he will claim me, and right now, at this moment, I am the luckiest girl alive.

To keep his legs in sight with my head bowed, I have to follow right behind him. We weave our way between the jeeps parked in the lot. The asphalt is hot and burns the bottoms of my feet, but I don't dare say anything. There are probably cameras filming everything. Instead, I roll my ankles and walk on the outside edge of my feet.

"Fuck," Alejandro says as he looks back to check on me. Then he squats down and heaves me over his shoulder and carries me to the door. When he sets me down, he says, "My bad, babe."

I stay frosty for him on the outside, but on the inside, I melt. He is not just a good man. He's kind too.

He lifts each foot like a horse farrier and examines the damage, telling me. "No blisters. Nothing a gob of aloe won't heal."

He looks me up and down, then swears. "You're too fucking gorgeous for your own good." He takes off his tank top and slips it over my head. It hangs off me, not hiding anything. It's so big, and he swears again. I lift the shirt, sticking my head in one of the oversized armholes, tie a knot, and make a toga coverup out of it.

He nods, pleased, then turns and walks into the building with me hot on his tail.

We enter into a club-like atmosphere. Using my peripheral vision, I absorb the layout. The first area is a small open bay with wood plank floors that spills into a more significant dance hall atmosphere. Alejandro walks right through without stopping. As we move into the larger area, he heads straight to the bar, and I catch a glimpse of a row of elevated booths on the opposite side. He orders a beer, two double shots of tequila, and a bottle of water. He keeps his back to me, and I maintain my obedient posture. I can feel the eyes of everyone in the room on me. But no one is talking. Not even murmuring. The only voices speaking are the men who file in and order drinks from the bar.

When Alejandro's order is filled, he slams back both shots of tequila, drains the beer, and then opens the water and turns to offer it to me. "Drink until I tell you to stop."

I lift my hands to take the bottle, but he slaps them away. I ball them up into fists and hold them steady at my side while I lean my head back, and he pours the water haphazardly into my mouth. I choke on the volume, spitting out the excess, and gulp down what lands in my mouth. It runs into my hair and down my neck, partially saturating the white t shirt.

I hear a few men chuckle and assume they enjoyed watching him nearly drown me, but it's equally possible they are enjoying the wet tee shirt view.

He returns the empty water bottle to the bar and walks out onto a covered patio deck that looks over a private lagoon cut off from the ocean by a row of huge boulders. I realize now why the ATVs were necessary. They are used to scale the height of the hill.

―――

Gabriel

―――

The Board hasn't convened yet, but all the pirates are here. Except for my crew, who are unloading and preparing the girls. My hand flicks over my knife as the men mill around, gaining observation points to ogle Marie. She's doing a good job trying to be invisible, but her beauty is a man magnet.

I scan the group. Most are pussy's just in it because it's the only way to make a living. Some are moderate badasses. They can kick the average dude's ass but aren't really violent. They do it for the money and the glamor. Then there are about ten who are hard asses like me that kickass because we like it. The more violent, the more rewarding the victory, and I top that list at the moment. Thus, the nickname: Barbados, the Brutal Barbarian. It's corny as fuck, but it serves the message to not fuck with me. Then there are the Wicked Ones. The ones that work directly under The King. They are evil and the ones I'm most concerned about.

After each raid, we meet here for an after-action debriefing. At least one of the Wicked Ones presides and reports back to The King. My mission objective was to discover who The King is and gather as much intel as I can on him. My goal was to become a Wicked One, enter his inner circle, and take him out myself.

But now that Marie's in the picture, I have to shift gears. I have to gather as much intel as I can quickly, then escape with Marie and leave the takedown of The King to the agency.

Finally, the door opens behind the upper-tier booths, and the Board walks out. The accountant, the doctor, the banker, and one Wicked One. They take their seats and look out over the crowd.

As soon as the Wicked One spots Marie, he stands and points at her. The crowd between us parts as I lead her to the center of the room. I glance at the door, hoping Roberto and my crew show up soon. I might need backup. Not that they are a guarantee, but I've tried to instill loyalty in them. That if we have each other's backs, we are stronger together.

When I stop, I stand stoic.

He asks, "Is she a gift for The King?"

"No."

"An offering to the Board then? Did you fuck up tonight?"

A few men laugh.

"No."

"Then why the fuck is she in here?"

"I'm going to keep her for myself as a spoil of war."

He laughs, "You are, are you?"

"To the victor belongs the spoils," I answer.

He grins. "Alright, you can keep her if you are the victor." Then he announces as he snaps his fingers, "But that applies to everyone. The winner gets this girl."

I pull my knife and crouch, reaching behind me for Marie. She puts her back to me, and I circle around her, explaining my position to the pirates. "Don't misunderstand. She is already a spoil of war. I am already the victor. She already belongs to me. If you think you're man enough to take her for yourself, then come and get her, motherfuckers. But I will kill those who try."

The Wicked One cackles, "This ought to be good."

# Eight

*Marie*

———

The blood drains from my face, and the spit in my mouth dries up. I look around the room at the men leering at me like I'm a piece of meat. Then I realize I am just a piece of meat to them.

Alejandro circles me with his knife drawn, prepared to kill and willing to die for me. I crouch down, matching his circling. I never thought I would have to use the grappling training that Cash made me learn, but I'm thankful I know it now. I will fight and kill to live, and I'm prepared to die trying. I strip the toga off, unhook my bikini top, setting my tits free, willing to use my secret weapon.

Cash said, "Little sister, never underestimate the paralyzing power that a pair of naked tits has over a man. Use whatever you have at your disposal to win."

Just then, Roberto, along with the rest of Alejandro's pirate crew, enters the bar. Each of them has two girls in tow. They are blindfolded, gagged, and their hands are bound behind their backs.

Roberto says, "Whoa! Whoa! Whoa! What the fuck is going on here?"

He parts the crowd and enters the circle of cleared floor space, followed by the rest of the crew, and they spread out, encircling us, becoming a human barrier. Alejandro stands, relaxed, and looks down at my naked tits, raises his eyebrows, and says, "Nice rack, babe."

Then he walks toward the Board while Roberto comes to stand next to me. "Like I was saying, she is already a spoil of war. I am already the victor. We had a record haul tonight. I'm claiming this one for myself. She belongs to me."

The Wicked One says, "So you are bringing us twenty-two and keeping one?"

"Affirmative."

He looks out over the crowd, and weighs his options, and decides it's better to give me to Alejandro and get us out of there before anyone else starts claiming girls for themselves.

"Very well. Have your second give your report." He waves dismissively.

Alejandro looks at Roberto, slaps him on the back, and says, "Give the man a full accounting. I'm going to take my spoil and get the fuck out of here." He nods to the men in the booths and says, "Gentlemen, please excuse me. I have a great need to do some fucking." He hunches his hips, frames his hard cock clearly silhouetted in his jeans, and everyone laughs.

Then he bends down, picks up his shirt and my bikini top, takes my hand, and we walk out the door.

---

Gabriel

---

Outside, I drag her to my jacked-up 4-wheel-drive Jeep Wrangler, not concerned that the asphalt is burning her feet. "That was reckless!" I shove her bikini top at her. "Those men are fucking animals. Why the hell would you show them your tits? Were you wanting them to fight for you?" I open the door for her and help her climb in, then I stomp around the front of the jeep and pull myself up. I crank the vehicle then peel out, slinging gravel and rocks.

She doesn't say a word. She simply stares straight ahead. I glance over at her a few times, but her expression hasn't changed. She's pouting. "Put your damn top on. That gorgeous rack is distracting as fuck!" I snap at her.

She comes alive. Sitting up, grabbing them, and says, "That's exactly fucking right, asshole! They are distracting as fuck. Try keeping your eyes on the road, motherfucker, while I play with them." She taunts me as she tosses them back and forth. "Tits are a woman's secret weapon. No man is going to take a knife and stab them. I wasn't asking for a fucking fight. I was fucking preventing one!"

I glance over, unable to keep my eyes on the road, then I slam on the breaks, and she has to brace herself on the dashboard. When we stop, I command her, "Don't fucking move. I'm coming to open your goddamn door like a gentleman and help you down. But, by God, once you're on the ground, I won't be gentle."

I throw the shifter in park, take the key out of the ignition, and bailout. She scrambles into the driver's seat and searches for the key. I open the passenger door and show it to her. "You're not going anywhere. You belong to me! Now, get your gorgeous ass and tits back over here and let me help you down."

"No!"

"Marie, that is not the right answer. If I have to come get you, I have no problem forcing you to do whatever I want, when I want, how I want, as often as I want, where I want." She cuts her eyes at me and sees the truth. This is not negotiable. She climbs back over, reaches for her bikini top, and I tell her, "Oh, hell no. You're not putting that on now. It's my turn to play with them and distract the hell out of you."

"Fine!" She spits.

I respond, "The correct answer from now on is going to be, Yes Sir, Mr. Daddy."

Her jaw falls open, and she shakes her head. "I am not saying that!"

I tilt my head and reach in, lifting her out of the seat. "Oh yes, you will, and you'll be happy to say it. I guarantee it."

---

*Marie*

---

The cocky son of a bitch carries me across the rough terrain, and it's pure torture. My bare tits are sliding against his bare chest. I swear he's stomping his feet just so they bounce against him. He stops under a tree with a low-hanging canopy and sets me down.

Pointing to a specific rock, he says, "Sit right there. Don't fucking move! Not a single muscle! If you do, there will be dire consequences."

I fold my arms over my tits, hiding them from him, and consider it. Then I capitulate, toss my hair, but say, "Fine!"

I don't feel like fighting anymore anyway. I'm tired, thirsty, and hungry. But I'm still mad he's pissed off at me.

I stomp over, plant my sassy ass down on the rock, and turn my back to him.

The view is spectacular! Picturesque, beautiful. Postcard worthy. We overlook the ocean. There's a village below with sailboats and yachts moving on the water, coming and going ... freely.

You can see forever here.

# Nine

Gabriel

---

Women! They talk too damn much, and apparently, this one can't follow simple fucking instructions even though she says she will! I stomp back to the jeep, angrier than I should be, but she put herself at significant risk. She has no idea how bad that could have gone down. If they had banded together, we would have both died. Me fighting to fend them off, and her getting gang raped. Thank God, they function as individuals and not gangs.

I grab a blanket and the cooler I packed earlier and walk back to my peaceful place, letting the stress go. As I approach, I'm thankful she's still sitting on the rock, and that just pisses me off again. I shouldn't be relieved she's done what I've told her to do.

I stop short to gather my emotions and shove them into my SEAL box. Then I walk around the rock, set the cooler down, and spread the blanket out. Without saying a word, I invite her to sit on the soft fabric next to me. Then I begin taking the cheese cubes and summer sausages out.

She stands and looks down at me, but I ignore her. Then she sits and watches as I take a beer, twist the top off, and drink it without offering her any, looking at the tranquil view. When I begin eating, she sits on the blanket and says, "I had your six. Don't be mad."

I wasn't expecting that. I take another long draw of beer, then look back at her. Damn. She's so fucking beautiful right now. Her pretty face is makeup-free; her unbrushed hair is a tangled mess hanging over those gorgeous ripe tits that make a man forget everything else when he sees them. She is right about that. Her long shapely legs casually stretched out.

I hand her my beer, then reach in the cooler and get another one. I twist the top off, enjoying watching her suck the liquid out of it. Then I hand her the fresh one and reach in and get another one for myself.

She smiles at me, and it feels like I'm the one forgiven. I offer her the cheese and sausage, and we eat in silence. When the food is gone, I lean back against the rock and watch the vessels floating across the water.

Marie pulls her knees to her chest, hugs them tight, and rests her head on them. She looks at me, though, and not the scenery.

After a few minutes, she repeats, "I had your back. Don't be mad. I wasn't being disobedient."

Hmm, it's a start. I finish off my beer. Then I look at her. "It wasn't necessary. It was reckless, and you *were* being disobedient."

She raises her head, tilts it, looks up, then licks her lips. I smirk. Apparently, that's a habit she has when she's pondering something, and it's cute as hell.

Then she looks back at me and says, "You're right. It wasn't necessary. I'm sure you can handle more than one man at a time. But you did tell me to stay on your six. Move when I move, I believe, were your exact words."

Her smirk is righteous, not sassy, but I raise an

eyebrow at how she is justifying what she did now, knowing that wasn't why she did it then.

Her expression concedes my point. "Okay, it was reckless. I'll own that."

She looks up again, "And you're also right in your perception of my obedience to your instructions." She looks me in the eye. "I did disobey you. But hear me out, please. I don't want you mad at me."

I look at her and wonder how she's gotten under my skin so deep, so fast.

"Those thugs saw an unbound, submissive woman walk in with you. I didn't want them to think that I would be submissive to them if they were stupid enough to challenge you. My disobedience wasn't to disobey your instructions. It was a demonstration to show them that they weren't going to win a submissive woman. They were going to get a fighter. I choose to be obedient to you, but I sure as hell wasn't going to be obedient to any of those motherfuckers."

Damn. That's the sexiest answer ever.

She shrugs, "The tits were thrown in just for the shock factor."

"Five," I tell her.

She frowns, "Five?"

"I can handle five in a fight."

She smirks, and the submissive girl asks for permission to snuggle up next to me.

I lift my arm, and she wiggles in, leaning her head back on my chest, relaxing as the people below come and go.

---

*Marie*

---

A hot gentle breeze blows, keeping the bugs at bay, and I get sleepy, listening to the even deep breathing of Alejandro. I start to close my eyes to drift off to sleep too, but then it hits me. I'm his captive! And he's asleep! I know I'm his captive, but I'll be damned if it doesn't feel like I have not a care in the world, snuggled up with him, enjoying the view.

My heart slips a beat, and I try not to change the rhythm of my breathing while I contemplate escaping. Can I get the jeep key out of his front pocket without waking him? And if I do, can I get in the jacked-up jeep without help? I sigh and close my eyes. Nope, and I'm really not sure I want to.

...

...

Mmm, that feels good. My nipple grows taut as little goosebumps break out as the sweet sensation of a warm hand cupping my breast lightly stroking it with the pressure of a feather arouses me from my catnap. I keep my eyes closed, enjoying the gentleness of Alejandro's touch as my senses wake. The soft, gentle breeze from the water caresses my body along with him as I become aware we are still sitting under the canopy of a tree overlooking a beautiful view. I relax and let him please me.

Maybe I'm wrong to be so docile. I'm sure I will be judged for it. But when a man like Alejandro wants you, even if he steals you, you would be a fool to resist him.

Mmm, that feels so good. I would be a complete idiot not to please him, and right now, he is pleasing us both. But I would be an even bigger fool not to relish his pleasing me.

He pinches the hard tip, twisting it between his fingers, and a powerful wave of sweet sensations surges over my body.

God, that's good. I move my head, slipping

down to lay on his lap, and let him have his way with me.

I peer up at him through my closed eyelids to enjoy his handsomeness while he plays. The bandana is gone, and his long, black hair hangs down. A small, pleased smile lightens the seriousness of his face. God! The man is incredibly handsome.

His hand continues to tease my tit while his other hand braces my head, lifting my weight off his lap as he slides his body out from under mine. Then he lays me gently on the blanket and stretches his incredible body next to me.

Leaning on his elbow, he continues to move his fingers with a touch as light as a feather over my skin. The softness has an incredible effect. My skin comes alive, and I feel nothing but desire for this man.

I open my eyes and reach up to touch him. He lowers his face, allowing my hand to cup it. As soon as contact is made, an overwhelming feeling of belonging washes over me, and despite the way, I became his, I know I am. I stroke his cheek, enjoying the rugged stubble, countering the tickling of his caress.

His eyes meet mine, and my soul reads his

soul's message. He is never letting me go. Not because he's a pirate, not because he's dominant, but because his heart belongs to me.

I wrap my hand in his gorgeous thick mane and pull his head down, needing his lips to kiss me. He allows me to bring him in, but he doesn't kiss my lips. He suckles my tits, making me moan, owning that I'm a woman wanting more.

As my back arches enjoying his attention, I see him rushing toward me on the deck of the yacht and know he was a hero coming in hot and not a pirate coming in cold.

# Ten

Gabriel

---

Her moans have the effect of a song of sirens over me. My promise to play with her beautiful tits to distract the hell out of her is backfiring on me. It was said in anger to torture her as payback to teach her lesson. I don't get even. I get ahead. But the more she moans to express her enjoyment, the more I want to please her, not punish her.

My tongue rolls her taut tip around and around, then flicks it, then sucks it. Her moans are growing more profound, and her body is beginning to move under me. Squirming with each sensuous sensory overload.

Her hands begin to move along my body, wanting to give me pleasure, asking me to give her more than my mouth, needing me to satisfy the growing ache inside her. But now is not the time. Now is not the place. This is just a promise that if she's obedient, this is what being mine will bring.

I lift my face from her breasts and look at her. Her eyes are hooded and partially rolled back in her head. Her jaw is slack, and her mouth hangs open with her lips forming a perfect O. My cock thumps despite my knowing I'm not taking this any further right now.

"We need to go."

Her hands pause, listening, then they try to keep me close, but I stand and offer my hand to help her up.

Her face is so beautiful, staring up at me with that wanton expression, not wanting to go, but she takes my hand and stands. I position her where I want her, then take the cooler and hand it to her. She hooks it under her arm and braces it against her hip. Hmm. It's heavy for her. I take the blanket by the corner and lift it, shaking it up and down, letting the breeze blow the sand off. Then I roll it up and reach for the cooler. We stroll back to the jeep, letting her pick her way along the ground.

At the jeep, I toss the blanket in, place the cooler on top, and look back at her. Her eyes are homed in on my ass, and she is totally drooling over it.

I pick her up and put her in the jeep. Her eyes are glued to me as I walk around and climb in. I tell her as I put the key in the ignition, "Put your top on. I don't need the distraction on this next leg of our trip."

She takes her top off the dash and hides her secret weapon from my eyes.

---

*Marie*

---

God! This man is ... all fucking man! I shift in the seat to watch him drive. His fingers are long and strong but have such a delicate, light touch. The way he handles the steering wheel is sexy as fuck, and my skin tingles where they touched me. His arms are powerful with thick veins, and I lick my lips, trying not to show him how turned on I still am. But damn, the ache inside is not going away anytime soon.

"Where are you taking me?" I ask.

"My place."

"I need some clothes."

"No, you don't."

I look at him. "I'm going to wear my swimsuit everywhere?"

"Not everywhere. My place."

"May I wear your clothes?"

He laughs, "Sure."

I look out the window, thinking about that. "So, what kind of place do you have?"

"You'll see."

We drive a few minutes, and curiosity gets the better of me. "What's going to happen to the other girls?"

"I won't discuss that with you."

"Why not?"

He glances at me. "No."

"You don't know?"

"I know. You don't need to know."

"Why not?"

"Marie," He raises an eyebrow, warning me to back off.

"Just answer me this one question, and I'll let it go. What happens if their family can't pay the ransom?" I ask.

He frowns but doesn't look at me and doesn't answer as he turns down an unmarked path and shifts the jeep into four-wheel drive to climb up the side of the mountain. The going is slow and scary. The ledge we are on is just big enough for one vehicle. I try not to think about the danger and just enjoy the view. It's even more spectacular from up here.

He pulls the jeep into a small cove cut out in the side of the mountain, where a small house has been built, shifts into Park, turns to look at me, and answers, "They aren't ransomed."

My mouth drops open, "None of them?"

He nods.

I stare at him as comprehension settles over me, but I have to hear him say it. "Why are they kidnapped then?"

He looks at me, and although he said I don't

need to know, he knows I can't let it go. "They are sold." He admits.

---

## Gabriel

---

The horror of my words hit her hard, and she stares at me like I'm the devil incarnate. "You're not kidnapping for ransom? You're a human trafficker?"

At that moment, I realize that if I let her believe that about me for one second, my image in her eyes, even when she discovers the entire truth later, will never recover from the damage done right now. She is never going to forget this moment, and I have to make a decision. Confess my undercover status and risk being exposed, which if I'm discovered will mean a tortured death or lose Marie forever.

It's an easy decision. One, fifteen hours ago, I would never have believed I would make.

"My name is Gabriel Managus."

She blinks, trying to hear what I'm saying through the bomb that exploded in her mind.

"I'm an undercover DEA agent. Let's go inside, and I'll explain what I can."

She nods, but as I walk around the jeep to get her, she begins to sob. I open the door, and she falls into my arms. I carry her inside as her body racks with the pain of what this means.

# Eleven

*Meanwhile, in-flight with thirty minutes to touchdown in the Virgin Islands ...*

———

Crockett

———

Zane calls in.

I turn to Cash, "It's our FBI guy." Then I walk to the back for privacy. Nina follows with a pair of earbuds for us to share.

"Zane. You have me and Nina. What did you learn?"

"A lot. This pirate ring is called The King's Crew. They were originally based out of Jamaica and dealt mostly in drugs and smuggling. But recently, they shifted gears and are now suspected to be heavily involved with human trafficking. The FBI suspects the old King was dethroned, and a new guy has taken over. Thus, the shift. Unfortunately, we don't have a lot of intel on the crew, but there is good news."

"Apparently, the DEA recruited a former SEAL by the name of Gabriel Managus. I don't know him, but Cash will probably remember him. Managus is the one who actually discovered the trafficking aspect. He has been deep undercover for six months. His DEA handler's name is Pete. Pete's going to pick you guys up at the airport."

"I spoke to him before I called. He let Managus have a long leash. Pete doesn't know where Managus stays. He was just interested in results, and apparently, Managus was moving up in the ranks fast. They were both hopeful Managus would get a meeting with The King soon. He told Pete he was leading the raid last night."

"Tell us about the raid. How did it go down?"

"There were no casualties. Managus himself

took out the captain, and he cold cocked him, and he was unconscious for hours. Everyone else was drugged. Get this, there were twenty-three girls onboard. It's the largest haul yet. The FBI is working on getting permission to take over the case, but it's not official yet."

"Copy that. What else did the captain say?"

"He shared that he held a gun on Managus but didn't shoot because one of the girls was with him. He identified her as Marie Daniels."

I look at Nina. "We need to know if Managus would recognize Marie."

Then I ask Zane, "How were the police notified and when?"

She takes her earbud out and goes to ask Cash. He sits up in the seat and nods, then looks back at me. She puts her hand on his shoulder and pushes him back down, but he gives me a thumbs up.

When she puts her earbud back in, Zane has shared that when the captain woke, he used a flare to signal another vessel. "Standard procedure. The yacht was boarded by the Coast Guard five hours after the raid occurred at 8:16AM."

"The radios were stabbed with a knife. Ingenious really. Quick, effective. SEAL tactics."

I tell him, "Send us the GPS coordinates of the yacht at the time of the raid and send me Pete's cell number. That's all the questions I have right now. Foxtrot?"

Nina adds, "Cash verified that Managus met Marie when he was in BUD/S. He is 100% positive Managus would recognize her. But he doubted Marie would remember him. She was around sixteen or seventeen when they met."

Zane says, "I'll pass this along. Listen, if you need me, just say the word. It's a four-hour flight from here."

"Good copy. I'll assess the situation when our boots are on the ground."

"Copy that," he says, then he disconnects the call.

Nina looks at me and says, "Cash feels much better knowing Managus is with her. But I'm not sure it's a good thing. She could blow his cover and get them both killed."

"Yeah, I know. I thought the same thing."

"Come on. Let's brief the others on what we've learned."

When we return to the front, I sit next to Cash as Nina prepares her briefing. While Meghan cues up Dark Thirty, our white-hat hacker, and License to Own, our overwatch drone operator on a Zoom call. When Nina's got the slide show ready, she looks to Meghan and gets the nod that everyone is present. Then she turns to address the team.

"Gentlemen, this is not a sanctioned FBI rescue mission. Currently, we are operating as Coq Blockers, so be mindful of the rules of engagement. We will be working directly with DEA Special Agent Pete Stanton. Our mission is to recover Marie Daniels. She is the little sister of our brother, Cash Cohen. He is here as a courtesy and not an operating team member."

She looks at him with her famous single-cocked eyebrow, and he doesn't refute her. Meghan pats his leg and whispers loud enough everyone can hear. "It's okay, sugar, you can hang with me. I'm the eyes and ears of everything that goes down."

He gives her a grateful look, so Nina continues the briefing.

That went down better than I could have hoped. I look over at Mike Franks, and he is grinning.

Nina shares the intel we have on our brother, Gabriel Managus, and Jocko raises his hand. When she pauses, he adds, "I know him. Lucifer and I were called over to work a mission with his team. He's solid."

She shares that twenty-three girls were taken in total but doesn't elaborate.

Justin Davis asks, "Are we expected to leave them behind?"

Nina looks at me and waits for my decision. Coq Blockers is my company. Therefore, it's my call. I stand to address them. "Freedom is never an option. Marie is our number one target for rescue. She's our priority, but we aren't going to leave a single girl behind. If we can't extract them with Marie, then we will ensure they will be rescued as soon as possible."

"Hooyah!"

Nina shows us on the map the location where the abduction took place and instructs Dark Thirty to pull the last 48 hours of satellite imaging of the area and comb it for the kidnapping to see where they took the girls.

She also shows us the beach bar where Managus and Pete's clandestine meetings took place. "This will be where Cash and Meghan hang out. The rest of us will set up at Pete's house. Any questions?" She looks around at everyone.

Brody asks, "What's his undercover name?"

The look on her face makes everyone laugh. "I'll get back to you on that."

Meghan tells her, "Alejandro Barbados."

Nina points to her and repeats his name.

Meghan bumps Cash's arm and winks at him. "See what I mean, sugar?"

At the airport, Special Agent Pete Stanton greets us with handshakes all around. "I've heard good things about your group. Let's hope the FBI sanctions this mission soon."

While we walk through the terminal, Pete confirms we are setting up our base of operations at his beach house. Nina smiles but doesn't say anything.

He shares much of the same information we already heard from Zane. Except that Managus has a check-in at the beach bar in the morning at 8:00 AM.

Nina tells us, "Keep that information on the down-low for the moment." She glances at Meghan, and with eye contact only, shares she has news. Meghan gives her a head-nod. Then she continues. "We need access to the police security cameras."

He says, "There isn't a lot."

She nods. "Guess we'll be scanning vacation footage then."

She looks at me. "Which means, good decision to bring me. Otherwise, your ass would have been in the doghouse forever!"

# Twelve

*Marie*

---

Sitting on the sofa inside the small one-room cottage, hugging a warm cup of tea with a shot of whiskey and a spoonful of honey in it, I can't believe what Alejandro, or rather Gabriel, has told me. But I know it's the truth. The story is too crazy to be a lie.

He started off saying he can't say much about it, but once he started, it was like a dam broke, and he wanted me to know everything about him. He talked about his SEAL training and Cash. He shared that he recognized me because he had seen me sitting at a table in Suds After BUD/S with my brother, and how he and a couple of his buddies came to the table to scope me out, but how protective Cash was of me and how he threatened their lives if they didn't leave me alone.

He shares his SEAL tours, how he came to work for DEA, how this assignment was supposed to be about drugs, but he learned the business was human trafficking. He confessed that it's the hardest assignment he's ever undertaken, and when he saw me, he knew he couldn't let that happen to me.

I set my empty cup down on the little table at the end of the sofa, unhook my bikini top, push down my thong, step out of it, and walk over to him, where he is sitting cross-legged on the floor. His beautiful amber eyes look up at me with the sincerest look in them, and I see the pain that he's endured throughout his life, sacrificing his own happiness for the freedom of others. He's done it all completely alone.

I reach my hand out, and he takes it. Staring up at me with eyes that are no longer thinking but feeling. I kneel down in front of him, place his hand on my tit, and tell him. "You had me when you boarded the boat."

Then I mount him and give myself to him.

His lips attach themselves to my tit, and he suckles for just a moment as his arms reach around me and pulls me down to sit on his lap. They kiss my skin, traveling up my chest to my neck and finally my lips. I cup his beautiful face as we kiss. His tongue enters my mouth, but instead of playing with my tongue, I suck it, and the moan that vibrates from his throat is my reward.

I release his tongue to place little loving kisses all over his face as his hands hold my body but do not move. He is lost in my love, receiving, not giving, and that is exactly where I want him to stay.

I push him over with my body, and he lays down, letting me take control. I unbutton his jeans, then push the zipper down. Then I reach around to his ass, and he lifts his hips for me to pull his pants off. I work them down while he watches. Glancing at him, seeing the deepness of his emotions expressed on his face, turns me on at a level I have never been before in my life.

When he's naked, I begin placing kisses up the inside of his legs, parting them as I move upward. When I reach his package, I lick his balls, then his cock from bottom to tip. His fingers slide around my head, then grip my hair, and he pulls my lips back to his. Gliding over the length of his body, my skin tingles with the direct connection. He stares into my eyes as I resist his kiss.

I spread my legs, raise my hips, and pull back. He lets me go, and I move to mount him. Taking his cock, I stroke my slit, wetting it, then I ease down onto it.

Our eyes never break the connection as I move, back and forth, up and down, fast, slow, deep, short. Watching his reactions, learning how to please him. He is a stallion, a stud, and I fuck him, trying not to cum, but I can't hold back.

I throw my head, tossing my hair wildly, and rock my world.

When I finish, I look back down at him, and he's smiling. Pure joy radiates from his face, and I tell him, "Yes sir, Mr. Daddy."

The look on his face is priceless, then he flips me over and proceeds to prove that I will forever gladly call him that.

---

Gabriel

Laying spent on top of Marie; I can honestly say I have made love to someone now. I give her a dismounting peck on her lips, and she smiles a lazy, satisfied smile. I pick her up and carry her to my bed, where she cuddles up with me, and we sleep until dark.

I wake first and lay thinking about how to handle the situation. I don't have to report to the King's for three days since I'm on a snatch and grab raid team. I play with Marie's hair absentmindedly. When I report on the fourth day, the group will be given the next targets. I'll assess the scenarios and put together a plan, but I don't want to get back in that rut. I need to take this opportunity to move to the next level of their organization.

Marie stirs, then rolls over to look at me. "Hey," She smiles and sits up on an elbow.

"Hey there," I smirk. Her hair is sticking out everywhere. She looks wild and untamed, but she's not anymore. I pucker my lips, and she leans over to kiss them.

"Umm, I'm going to like waking like this." I tell her, then ask, "Are you hungry?"

"Starving," she admits. "What is there to eat here?" She looks around my bare living quarters.

"Pizza, of course." I laugh and scoot to the edge of the bed.

She crawls up behind me, flings her arms over my shoulders, pressing her tits into my back, and says in my ear. "I need to use the ladies' room, but I don't see one."

I chuckle. "Now that is an issue since this is a bachelor pad." I turn to her, dipping my shoulder and pulling her into my arms. "I just step outside and take a whiz."

She lifts her eyebrows and says, "I'm going to have to go outside?"

I laugh, "Not exactly. There's a bathroom on the back porch, but don't expect much. It's just a toilet."

"Great!" She says as she slips off my lap and trots out the back door. Her ass cheeks rolling as she goes.

"Yep, I'm going to like waking like this."

# Thirteen

*Marie*

———

HE WASN'T KIDDING. THERE IS ONLY A TOILET with a curtain surrounding it for pretend privacy. I relieve myself, flush it, and pull the curtain back. He's turned on the exterior lights for me, and I look out onto a large lush green carpet, and in the moonlight, I see a waterfall in the distance.

This is paradise!

When I walk back in, he's still naked, lighting a candle on the small dinette table. The pizza box is already sitting on it. "I hope you like it with everything and aren't a pepperoni only kind of girl."

I giggle. "I'll pick off what I don't like." I walk over to my swimsuit and pick it up.

"No, ma'am." He shakes his head. "Naked."

"But...."

He turns to the small icebox, ignoring me, and asks, "Beer or water? I'm afraid that's all I have to offer."

"Beer, please." I walk over naked and sit down. He brings the beers, twists the top off, and hands one to me.

I take it, and lift it, and say, "Here's to prison being a paradise."

He smirks, and as I drink to my own toast alone, he flips open the box, takes a piece of pizza out, and eats it. Watching him consume it fascinates me. He takes enormous bites, chews maybe three times, and swallows. "Eat." He nods to the box. "I thought you said you were starving."

I shake my head and admit. "I was just fascinated watching you consume that piece nearly whole."

He smirks. "I'm starving. I had to share my midday snack with your hot little piece of ass."

I laugh and pull a piece of pizza out of the box.

Examine the contents on it, then eat it without taking anything off.

After two boxes of pizza are gone and eight beers, we're sitting outside on the front porch looking out over the water with the moonlight dancing on the surface.

"How did you find this place?"

He says, "It's a safe house."

"Oh, well, it is definitely isolated."

He finishes off his beer, stands, offers his hand, and says, "Let's go get a shower."

I take it, and he pulls me to my feet. "Please tell me it's the waterfall out back."

He grins. "It is."

"Awesome! Lead the way."

---

## Gabriel

---

Marie holds my hand and follows behind me as we walk across the small field that separates the house from the waterfall. I have two towels slung over my shoulder, a plastic bag with a bottle of shampoo and a bar of soap, my knife strapped to my leg, and a spotlight.

"Is the water cold?" She asks.

"It's not spring water. There's a holding pond that warms the water before it flows over the side. The temperature is nice. It's refreshing after a long, hot day."

When we arrive, I drop her hand, toss the soap bag in the pool, then cross over to the palm tree, where I hook the spotlight and hang the towels.

"WOW!" She whispers in awe as the area lights up.

On the opposite side, the water falls fifteen feet and lands on a flat rock shelf, then drains into a large pool. She walks to the edge and looks down, then cackles. "OH. MY. GOD! Is that me?"

I sprint past her and dive in. When I surface, she asks, "How deep is it?"

"It's about twenty feet all around," I tell her as I tread water. "Can you swim?"

"Yes sir, Mr. Daddy, I swim." Then she holds her nose and jumps off. She looks so young and carefree at that moment, and my heart rejoices being here with her.

When she surfaces, she's right in front of me. "God, this is amazing!" She twirls around in a circle, then she dives under the surface and comes up next to the waterfall.

I swim over to the soap bag, then swim to the steps. "There are stones just under the water here. Be careful swimming over." I warn her.

She leans forward, then does a dainty crawl along the surface to me. Good. She's a strong swimmer. I pull myself onto the submerged step and stand waiting on her.

When she arrives, she stares up at me, "You have the most beautiful body. It's sculpted perfection."

I laugh as I lean over and offer her my hand to help her up. "I don't know about that."

She takes it, and with one pull, I lift her straight up out of the water. As her beautiful body emerges, my cock gets hard again.

"Trust me." She clicks her tongue twice. "It's magnificent."

Then she takes the bag from me, opens the bottle of shampoo, and squirts half of it in her hair. She begins at the top, lathering it up into a thick white foam, then she continues, working it down her body.

I know I should bathe too, but I can't tear my eyes away. She moves like a squirming siren dancing, and my body teases with passion as my balls fill with semen. Watching her lather her tits and then her butt cheeks, draws me to her.

I spin her around to face me, bend down, and cup her ass in my hands, then lift her body off her feet. Her legs wrap themselves around me, her hands fall on my shoulders, and her forehead nuzzles mine as I carry her under the waterfall.

I lift her hips, spread her cheeks, and arch to enter her. Her velvety warmth seizes control, and I stand rigid while she takes care of us both.

---

*Marie*

---

Walking back to a tropical mountain hideout, after making love under a waterfall, eating passion fruit cut fresh off a tree, naked with my hair wrapped in a towel, next to the man of my dreams who is also naked with a towel draped over his shoulders, would never have made it on my bucket list, but it absolutely should be on everyone's.

"So, do you go by Gabe or Gabriel?" I ask as I take another bite from the fruit he offers.

"Neither right now. I'm Alejandro Barbados."

"Got it, but back home, what are you called?"

He smirks, "Hardass."

I laugh and reach around behind him and grab it. "It is pretty damn hard."

He chuckles. "Gabriel."

I smirk, "Too late. I'm calling you Hardass too."

He shakes his head, then rears back and throws the empty shell out into the field. A wild deer springs up and runs away.

"Oh, my gosh! He was right there!" I squeal, jumping up and down.

Whoosh!

I'm flat on my back, staring at Gabriel's face with his wet hair tickling mine. His lips begin placing little butterfly kisses all over, working their way down my body. Sending thrill after thrill through me as I stare up at the most exquisite star-filled sky. I must admit, getting eaten alive under a canopy of a billion stars tops the list of best things that have ever happened to me.

# Fourteen

Gabriel

---

Marie tries to buck my mouth off, but I hold her down, sucking her clit until her legs stiffen. Then I insert two fingers and call her orgasm, stroking her G-spot. She explodes with an uncontrollable fit of quivering.

Yeah, baby, I smirk as she collapses. You are never going to forget me.

I crawl back over her and hover, watching her reaction when she comes to. Her eyelids flutter, and then she takes a deep breath.

"Oh. My. Fucking. God!" She says and then opens her eyes and smiles at me.

"Don't move. I'll be right back." I wink at her.

"Don't worry. I don't think I can." She closes her eyes with an expression of sweet bliss on her face.

I sprint back to the watering hole, dive in, then climb out and sprint back.

She hasn't moved a muscle. I drop down next to her and peck her lips. "I'm back." My wet hair drips on her face.

She opens her eyes and blows the water back up on me. "That didn't take long."

"Speed and efficiency, baby, all rolled into one package." I tease her.

She giggles. "Will you carry me back to the house, please? I don't think my legs will make it that far."

As I pull her to her feet, her towel unwraps and falls to the ground. I ask her, "Cradled, over my shoulder, or piggyback?"

"Cradled. I don't think I can hold on at all right now." She shakes her hair out, then runs her fingers through it.

I bend over, grab the bag of soap, hand it to her, drape both towels around my neck, and then swoop her off her feet, carrying my girl back to the house.

I step onto the porch with her, push open the door, then turn my torso to maneuver her through the threshold.

"Where would you like me to set your majesty down?" I tease her.

She points to the bed, laughing.

"Perfect." I drop her, then fall next to her, laughing as we bounce.

I close my eyes as she asks, "What do you do for entertainment?"

"Sleep."

---

*Marie*

---

Laying on the bed, staring up at the ceiling, I'm not the least bit sleepy now. High as a kite from the most exquisite orgasm EVER, I roll onto my side and watch Gabriel sleep.

Although it's only been twenty-four hours, it feels like a lifetime. I guess it's because he's a

SEAL, knows my brother, and knew me. It's also because I've seen so many sides of him already. I've seen him as the pirate, a savior, a warrior, a provider, a lover, and a friend. I lean forward and kiss his skin. It's soft but firm. But the real reason is that what I feel for him is on a whole other level.

I've fallen for two guys before and thought it was love both times. The first one was just being in love with being in love. It was in high school and all about status and raging hormones. The other one was a good friend my freshman year of college that progressed to fuck buddy status simply to meet our needs. There weren't hard feelings when he phoned to tell me he was going out with someone.

But this with Gabriel is different. This is fireworks, and it's ... belonging.

CLANG! CLANG! CLANG!

Both Gabriel and I jump as the loud noise of a cowbell breaks the peaceful silence. He jumps out of bed. Unstraps his knife grabs his jeans, pulls them on commando, tells me to get dressed, straps the blade back on, and heads out the front door.

I run to my swimsuit and put it on as the headlights of a vehicle glide over the house. Then I run to the built-out closet next to the bed and grab one of Gabriel's shirts. Throw it on and look around for something to tie around my waist to keep it on. I spot a dog collar and leash hanging behind the door. I take the leather leash and wrap it around a couple of times, then hook the latch into the loop.

I walk to the window to see who is here. Standing off to the side, I peer around the sill. It's Roberto. He's talking with his head hanging down, and Gabriel is watching him with his hands on his hips. His body language is neutral, so I have no clue what's going on. But it can't be good because it's in the middle of the night.

---

## Gabriel

---

"Looks like he wants to see you."

"The King?"

"Yeah, man. The King himself." He hands me a sealed envelope.

I look at it. It's a simple white envelope. "Why do you think it's from The King?"

"Because The Wicked One gave it to me." He frowns. "That can't be good."

"You're worried because I took the girl?"

"Yeah. Some of the guys were bragging that you stole her from The King." He shakes his head. "It's either excellent news or really bad news."

I pat his arm. "Let's see what it says." I open the envelope and hold the letter in the car headlights to read it out loud. Honoring his loyalty and proving I trust him. "Alejandro, Impressive haul. Going the extra mile has rewards. But taking a prize without permission is forbidden. Report to the hangout at 9:00 AM. I will hear your request. Your King."

Roberto studies my face as I reread the letter to myself. "I'll call the crew. We'll meet you there."

I look up at him. "No. You guys weren't involved in my decision. I won't have you punished if that's what this is. Plus, if we show up as a crew, he might interpret it as a challenge to his authority." I look at the note. "Thanks, though, for offering, but I got this. It reads like he just needs me to ask his permission to have her."

He nods his head. "Okay, but what about the girl? Do you want me to guard her while you're gone?"

"You're the only one I would trust her with, but I'm taking her with me. It wouldn't look right if I don't bring her and ask him for her."

"But he may want to keep her."

"If he wants her, he can have her."

"You sure? She's pretty sweet on you," He looks up at the house, and I turn toward it too. Marie is standing away from the window, watching, twirling her hair around her finger. It's a nervous gesture. "Coming home to a willing woman in this business helps with the pain."

I press my lips together, hearing his confession that he's affected by it too, and I admit. "She is pretty sweet."

He offers, "I tell you what, I'll bring my baby mama to the hideout to eat breakfast around eight. Just in case."

I hold my hand out, and he takes it. "You're a good man, Roberto."

He laughs. "My woman keeps telling me that."

# Fifteen

*Marie*

———

GABRIEL STANDS WITH THE LETTER IN HIS hand, watching Roberto leave. Then he turns his head to look at the house. I walk to the window so he can see me. He gives me a head nod, then walks back.

"What's happened?" I ask as soon as he comes through the door.

He doesn't say anything. He just opens his arms, and I walk inside his embrace. He kisses the top of my head and says, "Sit down."

I sit on the sofa and hug my knees. While he

goes into the kitchen and takes the bottle of whiskey out of the cabinet. He pours two lowball glasses, then walks over and hands one to me. "Drink."

I take a sip as a lump in my throat begins to form. He slams his back, then sets the empty glass on the table and asks, "Did you not understand the word, drink?"

The lump in my throat forms fully with his stern tone. There's a slight frown on his brows, and his eyes are serious.

I bring the glass to my lips and slam the liquid back. It burns so much I lose my breath and cough.

He asks, "What's the right answer, Marie?"

I set the empty glass on the table and say, "Yes Sir, Mr. Daddy."

He says, "That is always the right answer; remember that."

I nod.

"I've been called out on taking you."

The blood drains from my face, and my spit dries in my mouth.

---

## Gabriel

Dammit. There was no easy way to say it. I pour us both another shot but wait before I tell her to drink it. I stare at the clear amber liquid running through the options before I speak.

"What does that mean?" She asks, unable to wait. "Are they going to punish you? Do you have to give me back?"

I smile at her. "You're forgetting I'm Gabriel Managus, a U.S. DEA Special Agent." I look out the window. "And I nearly forgot that too." I stand, "Come on. It's time to go home."

Her head tilts suspiciously. "Just like that?"

"Affirmative." I hold my hand out to her. She takes it, but she holds back.

"I don't understand." She frowns. "If it is that easy, then why didn't we leave yesterday?"

I look down on her as a rush of emotions crash my system, and I clamp my jaw to stifle them.

"Answer my question, Gabriel. Why didn't we go right away if it is that simple?"

"Truth is, I was selfish. I wanted one night with you. I have a rendezvous with my handler this morning at eight. I was going to take you in then, but I won't have time now." I pull her hand to help her stand, she resists me.

"Why not?" She eyes the letter I tossed on the counter in the kitchen. "What does the letter say? How have you been called out? What are they going to do to you?"

Her sweet, concerned expression is almost more than I can bear, so I look out the window until her barrage of questions is over. Then I simply state, "Marie, don't."

"Don't what? Care?" Her tone is hard. "Too fucking late, asshole! I'm invested." She pulls her hand out of mine, reaches for the whiskey, and slams it back. Another slight cough, then she says. "I'm not ready to go."

"It's not your choice."

"The hell it isn't. I'm an American Citizen, and thanks to you, I'm free to continue to make my own choices. I don't belong to Alejandro. You can't tell me what to do, Gabriel Managus."

It feels like I've been bitch slapped.

"Answer my fucking questions. There are twenty-two girls that won't be going home if I do."

I stare at the spitfire calling me out.

Impatient, she stands and looks at the kitchen.

"Fine. If you don't want to tell me, I'll read the letter myself."

I move to block her path. "Sit down."

She bows up like she wants to hit me, and I tilt my head, warning her that isn't a good idea.

"Sit down. Calm down. I'll tell you."

She sits, glaring at me. I look back out the window and scratch my scruff, thinking how to handle her. Should I tie her up and take her in anyway? I smirk. I can just see Pete's astonished face when I bring him an angry rescued woman.

I look back at the spitfire. Or do I actually bring her with me like I lyingly told to Roberto? I sit back down and pull my glass of whiskey to me. Preparing my words, I twirl it on the table for a few seconds, then I look at her. "This is a discussion. Not a decision."

She answers with a straight face. "Yes Sir, Mr. Daddy."

Dammit. That pushes my buttons. I lift the glass and throw the shot back. "Go get the letter. Come back here. Then read it and tell me what you think."

She practically leaps off the sofa and runs to retrieve the letter. Watching her, I realize what a special person she is. Her natural, messy beauty makes my dick hard. She's smart, and that's a huge turn-on too. But this feisty, fearless side that's brave enough to even contemplate going back into the danger zone to fight for the freedom of complete strangers speaks directly to my soul. Which is the problem. How do I risk losing her by letting her?

She plops back down on the sofa and reads the letter out loud. "Alejandro, Impressive haul. Going the extra mile has rewards. But taking a prize without permission is forbidden. Report to the hangout at 9:00 AM. I will hear your request. Your King."

She drops the letter in her lap, and when she looks at me, I realize I don't have a choice. If I take her to Pete, she will never forgive me, and I'll lose her forever anyway.

"The way I read it is you just have to make a show of asking him. He wants to be seen as giving me to you, not you taking me from him."

I nod. "That's the way I read it as well. But you're beautiful Marie, and there is always the chance that he will want you for himself."

"Well, if that happens, we will just have to fight."

I smile, despite the seriousness, remembering how she had my six and before thinking, I tell her.

"You are forbidden from using your secret weapons."

She smiles. "Don't worry. That tactic is only effective when a shock factor gives you a little more time to escape. I do wish I had some clothes to wear, though."

"Don't talk like you're going."

She gives me a look, then says, "Don't talk like I'm not!"

# Sixteen

*Meanwhile, en route to the bar to rendezvous with Managus ...*

---

Crockett

---

Nina calls in, and I put her on speaker.

"Dark Thirty located the satellite images and tracked the dinghy they used to escape in. I'm sending the GPS coordinates."

"Roger that."

"It appears they disappeared through a small

gap in a rock wall on the other side of this island. The image shows them coming out two minutes later in a tiny lagoon. Managus took Marie off alone. They disappeared for fifteen minutes, then reappeared on the other side of the mountain walking. There have to be caves and at least one tunnel large enough for some sort of motorized vehicle because of the distance they traveled in the allotted time."

"Good intel."

"Yes, it is. They walked a short distance, then into a local bar. GPS coordinates are being sent now. Over the next thirty minutes, a large group of men flowed into it. The last group of eight men came out of the same place as our targets, and they walked the kidnapped girls, gagged and bound, inside."

"When our target left, they got in a jeep and drove off, then stopped to eat."

"What did you just say?"

"You heard me right. They stopped and ate. From what Dark Thirty described, it was not hostile."

Jack pipes up. "Give us the details."

She says, "They were amorous."

"They were what?" Brody asks.

"They made out." Jack translates.

"So, it was consensual?" I ask.

She nods.

When they continued in the jeep, they drove to the adjoining mountain, traveled off-road to a single-vehicle path cutout on the side that ends in a very private, very secluded cove. Sending the last set of coordinates. They are still there."

"So, he's not on the way here?" Pete asks.

"They haven't left the cove."

I look at Pete. He shakes his head. "That's very unusual for Gabriel. He is a stickler for being on time."

"What about the other girls?"

"They were taken back into the tunnel."

"Okay, we're coming back. No need unloading here."

Nina says, "Copy that. I'll release the Ambassador and Cash to hang out."

"Good copy."

"Foxtrot out."

Franks speaks up first. "So Managus is AWOL with Marie."

"Affirmative."

"Do we consider him a hostile?"

"That's unknown at the moment."

When we walk in, Nina has taken over the sunroom overlooking the beach. She has two monitors set up displaying the same area. On one, she has circled the tiny lagoon, the bar, and the cove. On the other is a live feed.

We file in and take a seat on the floor, waiting to be briefed. Jocko goes to the cooler, tosses water bottles to everyone, pours Lucifer a bowl, and then comes back and sits next to me.

Nina starts with, "As soon as Dark Thirty gave us coordinates, we launched the drone. This is real-time footage. Our target is still in the cove."

Jocko requests, "Let's have the details on the lunch. I think it will give us some insight. The odds of Managus going rouge are nil in my book. He's as solid as they come. He's working a plan, and he thinks he's alone."

Nina answers, "The specific description was Managus carried her from the vehicle. It wasn't clear if she was injured. They stopped under a tree. She came out on one side while he went back to the vehicle for the cooler. Dark Thirty zoomed in on her. She was not injured. She was topless with only a thong on and barefoot. She sat on a large rock and appeared to be enjoying the view."

"No shit?" Mike says.

"When Managus came back, he ate. She talked. It appeared they had a spat. They drank beer. They both ate. They snuggled, then napped, then made out. They did not fuck, however. Then they left."

I look at Brody. "Profile that for us."

He says, "It's classic Stockholm syndrome, but the problem with that is she's not been his captive long enough. That's a long process of brainwashing. She simply trusts him."

"She's been around SEALs for as long as she can remember. Cash is fifteen years older than she is and given that she knows what the other girls are experiencing, whether or not she knows he's a SEAL, she is subconsciously aware of it and will likely do whatever he says."

Nina points to a current picture of Managus on the screen and adds, "He's a handsome fucker, too. That don't hurt either."

I look at her, and she says, "What? He is."

Just then, Justin points to the live feed. "They're on the move."

Nina says, "Dirk is inbound. He'll set the helicopter on the beach." She points outside. "Fly nap of the earth to the rocks. You'll drop in the water. Swim in through the gap. The lagoon is not guarded."

I stand. "Let's go."

When Dirk comes down the beach, he is less than twenty feet off the water in a Coast Guard Jayhawk. He sets it down, and we jump in. Then he picks it up and hauls ass.

While we were getting our gear ready, we watched Managus and Marie travel down the cliff and out onto the road. They turned toward the bar, not toward town.

Pete watched us pack our gear, then his phone rang while Nina got a text alert. He stepped out to take it while she read, "It's Zane. The mission is FBI sanctioned. We are going in as Born To Fight Task Force. We have a green light to rescue and recover everyone."

I called out the assignments. "Motherfucker and Danger, you two will locate and secure the other girls. Badass, Hammer, and Fastball will be with me."

When Dirk hovers over the drop point, we bail off and swim to the rocks. As soon as we enter the gap, the water gets shallow, and instead of swimming, we pull ourselves through. While Lucifer strokes it out next to Jocko. Before we leave the shadow, I scan the lagoon beach with a monocular. It is deserted, but there are two ATVs parked in the cave entrance.

We submerge again and pull ourselves to the beach, keeping the noise of splashing to a minimum. After we secure the empty cave, I key Nina on the earpiece. "Foxtrot. We're in. Coms will be in-op while we are in the mountain. Update on targets position?"

"They entered the bar ten minutes ago."

"Catch you on the other side. Rocket out."

# Seventeen

Gabriel

———

When we enter the bar, I have Marie on a leash. It was her idea to use the dog collar to hook her to me with the leather strap. I knew this girl was smart, but her idea was brilliant, and I couldn't argue with her logic.

She's wearing what she called a slouchy t-shirt dress that she made by tying a single gathering knot off her hip. It's baggy as fuck and shows nothing. Which is perfect.

On the ride in the jeep, she didn't hold her

hair, letting it fly in every direction, and it's tangled as fuck.

She looks a hot mess, and she's behaving meekly like a punished puppy, complete with new bruises.

"I'm not an actress, Gabriel. I don't want to fuck up and get us killed. If I'm bruised up, they'll assume you had to beat me to tame me. Fresh bruises will be convincing. They will set the tone. You have to!"

So, this morning, I tied her hands together, then strung her up on the back porch and fucked her from behind. I rub my fingertips together, remembering how every time I pinched her rosebud tip between them, she jerked, then begged me to pound her harder.

I got carried away and slapped her ass. She screamed, "YES!" So, I slapped it again, and she encouraged me to keep doing it.

What started off as just a means to an end ended up opening a door neither of us will likely be able to close. The controlled delivery of consensual dominance was a turn-on for both of us. Right before her orgasm, her legs stiffened. Then they started quivering again, and this time, when I thrust my hard cock inside her instead of my fingers, slamming it all the way to the hilt, bottoming out in her, she literally exploded and squirted all over the porch, and I did too.

Best damn fuck of my life.

When I let her down and unbound her, she was crying. I carried her to the pool, and she cuddled the whole way. She kept telling me, "Thank you."

I was at a loss for words. I don't understand tears to begin with, but when they are from a woman I care so deeply for, they were like knives in my heart. It was a crazy sensation. Her tears were stabbing me, while her thank yous were soothing me.

I eased her down into the cool pool, then held her until she stopped crying and got a firm grip on her emotions. Then I lifted her out of the pool, and we sat on the side, eating our fill of passion fruit. After that, we slept under the stars on the grass until the sun came up and enjoyed a beautiful sunrise together.

Walking back to the house with our fingers threaded together, her other hand held my arm so she could lay her face on it. I have never felt more cherished and appreciated before.

Looking at her blue marks now, I see them as

badges of courage from a brave woman for the rescue of innocents and know we have bonded on more levels than most couples ever experience. She and I are kindred spirits.

Strutting my hardass up to the bar, I order my usual two shots of whiskey and a beer. When the bartender brings them, he says, "Rough night, Alejandro?"

I nod. "Rougher than I like, but the bitch had to learn a lesson." I slam the shots back, then ask him, "Billy, I've been summoned this morning."

He says, "Yeah, I know."

"Is he here?"

"Not yet. You'll know when he arrives." He looks at me. "All the Wicked Ones are required to travel with him."

"Perfect." I roll my eyes. "Nothing like a crew of psychopath pirates to deal with first thing in the morning."

He chuckles, reaches for the whiskey bottle, and pours me another shot. "This one is on the house."

I slam it back, then take my beer and scan the area, looking around to see how many men in the crowded bar I know.

The only one I recognize is Roberto. He's eating a platter of eggs and pancakes with his wife. He has his back to the door, so he's facing the booths.

I check my watch. We still have ten minutes, so I stroll out onto the patio to wait. Completely ignoring Marie as planned, she follows meekly like a punished puppy with her eyes down. I notice some bastards checking her out, so I give them a direct hardass stare. They all look away, except one. He gives me an approving head nod. I disregard his gesture, but yank Marie to me by the leash, grip her jaw with my hand forcing her mouth open, and give her a suffocating kiss. She kisses me back, hungry for my tongue, and I give it to her to reassure her. When I release her, I tell her, "Good girl," and a flash of I-dig-hearing-that flashes in her eyes, then she resumes the pitiful puppy persona.

Damn, that was hot! I smirk as my cock hardens, then turn to look at the dude and give him a wicked grin. He gives me another more respectful head nod, then looks away.

## *Marie*

---

I had no idea I was this kind of woman! None! If you had told me that I would love being spanked by a man, I would have laughed in your face. But ... I do. I so do!

Every step I take, my bruised, spanked ass responds with a little "hello," and it's making me wet. Avoiding eye contact with Gabriel is a must because I don't think I can hide my love for him. His kiss just then, followed by his 'Good girl' comment, made it pounce out of my eyes, and that's dangerous.

I close my eyes, and my throat tightens. This 'adventure' is about to come to an end, one way or the other, and the thought that he won't be a part of my future is really what has me terrified right now.

If The King takes me, Gabriel will be dead, and it won't really matter what happens to my body because my heart and soul will be shattered into a million pieces. If The King doesn't take me, I will stay with Gabriel for a bit longer, and that's my goal for this meeting. To be precisely what The

King doesn't want. To be the reward Alejandro desires.

After that, who knows what will go down. There are too many moving pieces on the chessboard to worry about.

I still don't know what lies ahead, but I'm content right now to live in the moment.

# Eighteen

Crockett

---

In the cave are two tunnels. One has ATV tracks. The other only footprints. Motherfucker and Danger enter the one with the footprints while the rest of us push the two ATVs up the tunnel far enough the sound shouldn't filter into the other tunnel. Then Hammer drives one with Badass on the back. While I ride behind Fastball, who places Lucifer over his lap.

Once we reach the entrance, we park them alongside the others there. Badass bails off and begins removing keys from them. While the rest of us access the outside. There's only one small footpath leading out.

I key Nina on the com, give her an update on the tunnels and the location of Motherfucker and Danger.

"Be advised, one." She says, "a black SUV just pulled up to the bar. The six heavily armed men that Nina warned us about are standing around it. We have eyes on our target. She's on the patio. She's wearing a dog collar and hooked to ..." She pauses, "*our* inside man with a leather leash."

"Copy that," I respond as my guys give each other looks that say, what-the-fuck?

Badass keys the com, "That behavior indicates that, at the least, the bar is a known gathering place for deviants. But it is most likely a BDSM bar, and they are working that angle."

Nina states. "He just kissed her, and ... well, there are fireworks between these two. You can't fake that kind of connection, and they are using the BDSM angle as cover and keeping her close, submissive, and compliant."

"Good copy," I answer. "Rocket out."

I wave us forward. Moving down the trail quickly, we're ready to evade any oncoming foot traffic, but no one is around. When we see the bar, we step off the path and take cover to observe.

The six men heavily armed that Nina warned us about are still standing around the black SUV. They are all wearing white jeans and Columbia-style beach shirts in various pastel colors. Their black weapons are drawn and brazenly contrast against their clothing. They aren't hiding anything. They are carrying openly.

Badass whispers, "This is the pirate's hangout. They are comfortable enough to open-carry."

I nod, understanding that the occupants inside are most likely part of the pirate crew, which will mean we must assume everyone will have weapons.

"What's the call?" Hammer asks.

"You and I will take sniper positions using the patio. Fastball, Luce, and Badass will enter and mingle. Watch and observe. We'll take them when they exit but protect them if they are threatened."

"Roger that."

Hammer and I leave them stripping down and unpacking the vacation apparel from their dry bags to mix and mingle.

## Gabriel

What the fuck? I flip around and put my back to the entrance while I gather my wits. Jocko Malone and his K9 Lucifer just walked through the damn door and another SEAL is with him.

I look around out over the landscape and think like a SEAL on a mission. If I were the sniper, where would I set up?

I'll be damned! Cash didn't waste any time calling in a favor. I spot not one but two. I grin. The odds just turned in our favor.

I turn back around and watch Jocko and his teammate sit at an empty table by the door. The distance between us is significant enough to chance eye contact, so I wait until he's finished scanning and accessing the crowd to look at him. When I do, he gives a slight head nod, and I return it, then lean down and whisper in Marie's ear while I play with her hair and squeeze her tit.

"Cash has sent the calvary, baby. We're going to take this motherfucker down today and save the girls." As soon as I said her brother's name, her eyes jumped to mine and are glued here. But instead of relief, I see the need to support the fight, and I want to nip that urge in the bud. "When the shit hits the fan, you are to fall face down on the floor and do NOT move. Play dead. Do you understand?"

She opens her mouth and answers my question correctly. "Yes Sir, Mr. Daddy."

I lean over and kiss her lips. "Good girl."

Just then, The King and his entourage of goons enter the establishment. He's an older, gray-haired man with big bushy eyebrows that need trimming. He walks in the middle of his six men. They are shielding him from anyone hostile as he makes his way to the center elevated booth. When he's seated, his six disciples come out of the crowd, one by one. I can't believe I missed them. They take their places on either side of him, and then he makes a fatal error.

He stands and proclaims to the crowd who he is and tells them he has a management situation to deal with, then he calls me forward.

"Alejandro, come and beg for forgiveness, and bring that bitch to The King. She belongs to me."

If he had said anything else, I would have played the game as scripted, but begging for forgiveness is never going to happen, and neither is handing over Marie.

I look at Marie's bowed head. She's still in character.

Then all hell breaks loose. Roberto jumps on top of the table and shouts, "Viva, our King!"

The entire bar romps. Everyone stands and begins stomping, taking up the chant. I'm not sure if this is an enthusiastic crowd of supporters or a rebellious distraction on my behalf, but I take the opportunity presented. Squatting down in front of Marie, I tell her, "Time to go home."

She jumps in my arms, wraps her legs around my waist, and we bale over the side of the patio railing and shimmy down the support poles to the ground.

I set her down, cup her face in my hands, and stare into her eyes, "Before anything else happens, I want you to know that I'm in love with you. You're my soulmate."

# Nineteen

*Marie*

---

Those amazing amber eyes pierce me to my core when he looks at me with that crazy intensity, but it's his words that just rocked my world.

He hoists me over his shoulder so he can run with me, and he sprints around the building to the parking lot. When we arrive, he sets me next to the jeep and says, "Get in. Keep your head down."

Then he retrieves three guns and heads back inside. I call after him, "YES SIR, MR. DADDY!"

And he throws up a hand in acknowledgment.

The first thing I do is remove the dog collar,

then I sit patiently and wait. My thoughts bounce back and forth from worrying whether Gabriel's okay inside or not and plans for our future together.

After thirty minutes or so, a large force of police arrives, with sirens and lights blaring. They fill the parking lot and then swarm inside.

A man with a badge around his neck gets out of the police chief's car and walks over. I spool the window down, and he says, "Marie, I'm Special Agent Nolan. Pete." He smiles. "This is Police Chief Hollis. Are you injured?"

I shake my head. "No, sir. I'm fine."

He nods and looks to the Chief. 'Okay, let's go inside." He turns back to me and says, "I'll send Gabriel right out."

"Thank you!"

---

## Gabriel

---

Pete escorts the Chief of Police in and introduces us while his officers are busy arresting people. I, in turn, introduce Malone, Black, and Roberto.

He asks, "What the hell happened in here?"

"A Pirate War broke out," I tell him, then I give him a quick summary. "There was a rebellion within the ranks. The new King shifted the focus from drugs to human trafficking, and the crews weren't happy about it." I put my arm around Roberto's shoulders and tell them. "This good man lead the rebellion. He's willing to testify in exchange for immunity and witness protection for him and his family."

Pete shakes his hand and says, "So you're Roberto. Gabriel spoke very highly of you throughout his assignment."

Roberto says, "Dude, I had no idea he was DEA. I thought we were going to roust the King from his throne today and install Alejandro."

Everyone laughs.

"I'll be outside in my jeep," I tell them. Pete pats me on the back and says, "Go. I got this."

Marie throws the jeep door open and bails out of the vehicle when I walk out the entrance. Watching her sprint to me with a huge smile on her beautiful face, radiating pure happiness, crushes my SEAL box of emotions, and they pour out.

When she throws her arms around me,

wrapping her body around mine, I bury my face in her tangled hair and breathe in her essence. She holds me so tight; I know I will never be lonely again.

---

Crockett

---

When the police finally arrived, Hammer and I climbed down from our position. Nina has been giving us updates from the drone from what she could see.

"Be advised. The lovebirds have flown south to the cove."

As we walk around to the front of the restaurant, four ambulances arrive and a tour bus. Jocko and Brody are walking out of the front entrance. As the four of us cross the parking lot, intending to go check on Mike and Justin. Jocko scoops up Lucifer and cradles him like he's a baby. "Is he okay?" I ask.

"He's fine. He's a happy boy. He got two of them today. Didn't you, my man! Who's a good boy?" He says in a totally out-of-character goo-goo voice.

"Why are you carrying him then?" Jack asks.

"Take your shoes off, and you'll understand. The fucking asphalt is hot."

Jack ruffles his fur and tells him. "My bad, boy. Logan and I know what to get you for Christmas this year."

Jocko laughs. "That'll be a photo opportunity."

Just then, Mike's voice keys our comms. "It's been a good day, tater. Y'all don't worry about Danger and me. We can handle these twenty-two beautiful young ladies, all by ourselves."

"Fabulous!" I answer. "We're at the end of the trail, waiting with ambulances."

Nina responds. "Celebration beach party tonight at Pete's."

"Hooyah" fills the air.

With Mike in the lead, on point, and Justin bringing up the rear, covering their six, the girls file by us. Each of them says, "Thank you!"

And our response is, "You're worth it."

The paramedics begin checking them out, and we walk back over to the bar.

Nina tells us. "Harness up, boys. Dirk's en route to retrieve you. He thought you guys deserved a treat, so he'll be serving up a Special Patrol extraction for your viewing pleasure."

The response is immediate. "HOOYAH!"

The last transmission from Nina is, "License, please return the drone to the beach house. I will handwrite the lovebirds an invitation for tonight's celebration for you to deliver before you sign off. I'm sure they will want to join us. I don't think anyone told them Cash's possessive ass is present, and if they want to keep that little piece of paradise a secret from him, they best be present and accounted for."

Dirk arrives, hovering over the parking lot, the flight crew chief tosses out the SPIE rope, and we hook the D-ring on our carabiner harness to it. Then he lifts us straight up, and the ride back to the beach house is absolutely spectacular.

This is the best job ever!

---

Gabriel

---

"Well, that's it," I tell Marie as I zip my duffle bag. "I'm packed and ready to go. The only thing left is to clean out the refrigerator."

She strolls over and opens it, peering inside. "There's only beer and pizza in here." She laughs.

"The bare necessities." I come up behind her and slide my arms around her. She leans back against me and sighs.

I kiss the top of her hair. Then unable to stop, I kiss her neck. She leans her head over, exposing it for me, and I brush her hair off it. Cleaning the path for my mouth, and I suck then nip the soft skin of her neck, behind her ear. Placing little hickeys as I work my way down, then along her shoulder.

Her hands reach around behind her ass and cup my balls, then she turns around and drops to her knees. Preceding to deliver a mind-blowing head-job. My balls begin to tighten up, and my legs stiffen, but before I explode, I pick her up by her hair. Pinning her body against the refrigerator, I slide my hands down her arms, thread my fingers through hers, lift them over her head, stretching her to her tiptoes. Then I transfer her left hand so that I clasp both her hands with one. All the while, I place kisses all over her face. Forcing her to keep her eyes closed. Then I grab her tit and pinch her tip. Knowing how much she likes that. She flinches, then her eyes open, and the fiery passion that flashes in them sends shivers down my spine. My hand falls to check how wet she is. But I already know. She's oozing, ready, aching for my cock. But I slide them in her anyway, tickle her g-spot, then pull them out to saturate her with her own juices from front to back.

The intense, fiery passion in her eyes shifts to hooded lids with lustful longing, and that look is what I want to see when I ram my cock so hard, so fast, so deep, that the refrigerator moans with my penetration.

---

*Marie*

---

Gabriel's thrusts are so fierce, we're rocking the refrigerator, but I can't get enough of him! Then his mouth is on mine, and he's fucking both ends at the same time. My eyes roll back in my head. I no longer exist as a single being. We are one, and when he explodes inside me, my orgasm falls helplessly from my body, united with his.

---

Gabriel

---

When we pull up at the address in the invitation the drone delivered, Marie shifts in the seat to look at me and says, "Cash can be intimidating."

She looks so cute, worried about her big brother bullying me, that I chuckle, "How many boyfriends have you warned about him?" Then before she can answer, I assure her, "That is not an issue."

She laughs and says, "I can't believe I said that. Force of habit. Sorry. He's just such a ...."

I touch my finger to her lips and silence her. "Hardass?"

She grins, "Yeah, but his nickname isn't hardass."

I give her a reassuring wink and tell her. "There's only room for one of those in your life at a time, and I claim that position from now on."

# Twenty

*Three months later at the Chicken Ranch.
Coq Blockers, Inc. Headquarters
in Las Vegas, NV ...*

---

Gabriel

---

"Cash, are you coming?" Meghan calls into the kitchen.

"Yeah, babe. On my way." He winks at us, stabs another bite of steak off Marie's plate as she battles him for it with her fork. "I've convinced her

I don't know how to ride a horse, so I'm getting riding lessons. She insists it's an employment requirement to be part of the team."

She appears in the doorway with a riding crop in her hand, tapping it against her palm. "You better hurry, 'cause I'm itching to use this on one of you."

He laughs as he struts in his cowboy boots towards her, confident that it won't be him. She smirks up into his face and says, "Don't push your luck! I will do it!"

He laughs down at her and says, "You'll try, but you won't be successful."

She giggles as she turns around, and they walk away, heading to the stables. "But it'll be fun being denied." Then she calls over her shoulder. "Marie, you have the controls. We'll be back when we get back."

Then Cash calls over his shoulder, "Gabriel...."

But he doesn't get to finish. Meghan interrupts him, "NO!"

When they're finally out the door, and we are alone, Marie rubs the inside of my thigh and says, "I bought a new flogger for my birthday. It's a beautiful deep purple suede. I can't wait for you to wield it."

I lean forward and kiss her lips. "Anything to keep my girl satisfied. I have something for you too. Do you want it now or later?"

She jumps up, forces herself between my body and the table, straddling me, her tits pushing into my chest as she wiggles on my cock. "Give it to me now, baby."

I chuckle, "Not that."

"But everyone is gone. We have the whole place to ourselves for at least two hours. We could christen every surface in my office." She teases me, tracing her fingers across my lips, knowing I like it.

"I meant I have something to give you."

"Oh, yay! I love presents. Give it to me now."

"Okay," I pick her up off my lap and push the chair back. "It's in my truck. Let me go get it."

She grins and says, "Hurry. I'll be in my office waiting for you."

I slap her on the ass, then go to the truck and get her present. When I walk into her office with the box, butterflies flutter around in my gut.

"Hang on. I want to record your reaction," I tell her as I walk over to the credenza behind her desk and use two books to prop my phone up. "Stand right there, babe." I check to make sure the camera is recording, then walk over to her and hand her the box.

She takes it and shakes it. The contents inside bang a little against the box. "Is it a controller?" She asks because the one she plays Call of Duty with is showing signs of wear.

I bend down and put my face in front of the camera, smirk and answer, "Sort of."

"I really need one."

I laugh and tell the camera. "No words truer have ever been said."

She rips the paper off, and I look back at the camera and comment. "Here we go!"

She holds the box out and frowns, smiling, and asks, "It's not a controller?"

I laugh. "It's not a video game controller. Open it."

She unfolds the box and then dies laughing when she sees the contents. It's a coffee cup with the words, "Yes Sir, Mr. Daddy" printed on it.

I tease her. "Just a reminder, so you start each day off with the right answer."

She says, "I love it!" Then she pulls out the matching t-shirt rolled up inside, giggling, and asks,

"And the matching shirt is a reminder for the rest of the day?"

"Oh, absolutely!" I tease her. "I don't want you to forget."

She leans her head back and falls forward on my chest. I give her lips the peck she asks for, then I say, "Try it on. I want to make sure it fits."

She says, "I don't think you can return custom printed t-shirts." Then she looks at the tag, checking the size, and the shirt unrolls. A small item falls out and lands on the floor.

"I got it," I tell her as I drop to one knee to retrieve it, then I hold it up and present it to her. "Marie, will you marry me?"

The stunned look is priceless, then she dies laughing, and reaches to help me to my feet. "Yes Sir, Mr. Daddy! I will marry you!"

I stand, taking her into my arms, and whisper on her lips. "That is always the right answer."

# Epilogue

One year later
Flying in to Las Vegas, NV ...

Gabriel

"Ladies and gentlemen, this is your Captain speaking. We will be arriving at our destination as scheduled. Mother Nature has blessed us with clear, sunny skies for the remainder of our flight. The temperature when we land will be a pleasant eighty-five degrees. Our cruising altitude will be ...."

Crockett takes the seat next to me, "Dirk said, 'She's a natural. She has a soft touch on the controls.'"

I smirk at him. "Yeah, man. She sure does."

He chuckles at my innuendo. "Newlyweds!"

Nina peers over the seat and states, "She seems to be content too."

I tilt my head and ask, "Why wouldn't she be?"

She and Crockett exchange a look before she says, "Well, she gave up her dream to join us."

I nod, understanding now what's she's implying. Marie's plan for her life before she lost her friends in the automobile accident was to become an airline pilot and travel all over the globe. I nod and explain my girl's new perspective. "In her words, not mine. That was just a selfish dream without purpose. This is her destiny."

Nina's eyes confirm there is no lingering doubt in her mind that Marie is indeed content, and she shares, "It is the most rewarding thing I've ever done."

Logan Black leans up from the seat behind me and adds, "That's true for me too. Nina, Jorja and I are discussing a last-minute change to the speech. Would you mind giving us your opinion?"

"Sure. No problem." She answers and leaves her seat to join Logan.

Crockett pats my knee, then stands and says, "Good to know, brother."

I look out the jet window watching the wing cut through the clouds, remembering our first outing as a couple. We were sitting outside Pete's house in my jeep, and I had just informed Marie that I was now the top hardass in her life when Cash rushed out of the house.

My first thought was he's coming to beat my ass, because well, I was fucking the little sister he warned me to stay away from, so I opened the door and stepped away from the jeep. If we were going to fight for her, we would do it on equal ground. But then I realized tears stained his cheeks, and the only thing he wanted was to hold his little sister to assure himself she was alright. It tore me up watching them hug.

I glance across the aisle at him, stretched out asleep. Those two are tight, and I'm thankful for that. Marie might not have trusted me if they weren't, and things would not have turned out as they did.

That night when we went inside Pete's house, we met the rest of the team, and I was impressed with their operation. Crockett, as team leader, began the debriefing with a toast to me. "To Gabriel. A man not only on a mission, but a man committed to the mission. If you ever decide to leave the bureaucracy of Government, Coq Blockers will hold a spot open for you."

"Hooyah!" The team said as one.

"Coq Blockers?" I laughed. "You're fucking kidding me?"

Crockett said, "Negative. Suits us, don't you think?"

Nodding my head, I answered. "Fucking perfect."

Then he asked me to recap my undercover assignment from the beginning, and I did, sharing some chilling stories. The more I talked, the more everyone became invested in the telling, totally tuning in, and I talked for almost three hours.

We capped the evening off watching the brawl from the interior security cameras in the bar. My crew of loyal pirates took on The King's men in a free-for-all fight. It was total chaos. There is no way I could have protected Marie.

Cash asked, "How did you manage to survive that?"

Marie answered, "We bailed off the patio deck in the back when Roberto jumped up on the table."

He looked at me, reached his hand out, and as we shook, he said, "Thank you for saving her."

The expression on Marie's face afterward and that piercing look in her eyes when I looked down at her was everything a man desires from a woman.

Then she looked back at the monitor and asked, "Did anyone get away?"

Brody answered. "Negative. We caught every one of them."

Jocko laughed, patting Lucifer's shoulder as he rolled over with his paws in the air, wanting belly rubs. "A few tried, but the fur missile took them down, and Badass and I dropped the others."

Then Brody clarified for her. "We were outnumbered, so we just stacked up a few lifeless bodies in front of the exit door and sent a clear message. There was no escape."

Then Jack summed it up, "Marie, if you're going to defeat evil, you have to be meaner than it."

She answered with, "The only thing necessary for the triumph of evil is for good men to do nothing. Edmond Burke."

The buckle your seatbelt sign lights up, and Marie says over the intercom, "Please buckle your seatbelt and remain in your seat until the jet has landed. We hope you have enjoyed your flight with Coq Blockers, Inc. and will fly with us again."

I smile. She's an amazing woman.

---

*Marie*

---

I reach for my glass of water to hydrate. The air in Vegas is a different kind of heat. At the conference of law enforcement officers, the speaker has introduced our company, and Logan steps up to the podium. "Good evening, my name is Logan Black, and I was a victim of human trafficking."

As she gives the speech that Jorja, Jocko's wife,

wrote, I glance around the table at this special group of people that have come together to continue the fight for freedom, and I thank my lucky stars that this company exists. Although Gabriel was my onsite hero and saved me, this amazing group of people came to my rescue without hesitation, then welcomed Cash and me into their fold.

When they learned I wanted to be a commercial airline pilot, Crockett called Aurelius Moore, the CFO. Then Coq Blockers offered me a pilot position. I couldn't believe it. I joined the team immediately. Dirk Sam was my instructor, and now I have earned my wings.

I glance over at Crockett and Nina, then around the table at Jack, skipping over the empty seat where Logan will join us. Everyone is listening attentively as she gives her accounting of being kidnapped and rescued. She ends with an encouraging reminder, "In the words of our founder, Jeff Crockett," she points out into the audience, "freedom is always worth fighting for, and Coq Blockers have taken up the fight against sex traffickers."

Applause fills the room, and Jeff stands to take

a bow. When he sits, silence settles back over, and everyone tunes back in. They are anxiously awaiting the main speaker. Logan's voice takes on the tone and manner of an emcee as she says, "He is a living legend. In service to his country as a DEVGRU Navy SEAL special warfare operator, he was the recipient of the Silver Star for valor in combat and the Navy Distinguished Service Medal for exceptionally meritorious service in a duty of great responsibility. As a DEA special agent, he succeeded in taking down the oldest known gang in the Caribbean, The King's Crew. He is a true hero. He's been called many names. His SEAL brothers call him, Hardass. His wife calls him, Mr. Daddy." She pauses with the laughter, and I graciously wave, understanding that the laughter is because every man secretly wants his wife to call him Mr. Daddy. Then she continues, "The Virgin Islands' inhabitants called him Alejandro Barbados. His pirate crew called him the Brutal Barbarian. It is my great honor to introduce to you Gabriel Managus."

She turns, sweeping her hand in a welcoming gesture. My beautiful man with his majestic muscles, black cropped military cut hair, a trimmed neat goatee, gives me his beautiful bright white smile, and nods at the standing ovation he receives. Then he takes the podium in his hands, squeezes it, flexing his magnificence, and the crowd sits and goes silent. He pierces them with his amazing amber eyes and states, "Freedom is not an option!"

Thank you for reading TARGET MARIE.
I hope you loved Marie and Gabriel's love story.
Review link: TARGET MARIE

The next book in the
A FEW GOOD MEN series is

## TARGET BELLA

I'm the youngest Navy SEAL to make DEVGRU / SEAL Team 6 / Tier One in over a decade. The benefits far outweigh the disadvantages on most fronts, but not where my love life is concerned. Girls my age are immature brats. They have no respect for the sacrifices SEALs make. Nor the commitment required. My team comes first. It's as simple as that.

So when I spot a possible 'Frog Hog' on the hunt at Suds After BUD/S Bar who is gorgeous and older by at least a decade, I hit on her, and she flirts back. Giving as good as she gets in regards to smart ass banter.

I like her immediately. She just might be what I need to survive my high-stress lifestyle. So I persuade her to take me home for a hookup. It wasn't easy, but it wasn't difficult either. No commitment. No strings. Just hot and heavy, balls to the wall ... banging.

The next thing I know, Bella Rayne Parker has become a bad habit too good to give up. And I'm fighting my feelings to stay frosty with her.

I've learned she lives in the shadows, hiding from someone. She's cautious and careful. Insisting on clandestine dates. But she's always punctual.

Until now.

When she doesn't show and leaves me in the dark, my gut tells me she's in trouble. I vowed to stay frosty with her, and I will, but only until I find her. When I do, that shit ends. Love isn't something you control.

Whoever has taken her will find out how fierce passion can be when I unleash my feelings and deliver justice so she will never have to live another day in fear for her freedom again!

## **PROLOGUE**

---

*Bella Rayne*

---

Y<small>EARS AFTER</small> I <small>WENT INTO HIDING...</small>

---

"Hi, Mick," I speak to the *Suds After BUD/S* bartender as I take a stool.

He walks up to me, "Hi, Bella Rayne. Your usual?"

"Yeah, make it a double, though," I tell him as I look down the length of the bar to the small group of men playing billiards in the area just off the large dance floor. "I need it tonight."

"You got it." Mick acknowledges as he turns around, opens the cooler, reaches inside, and removes a chilled bottle of Crown Royal Regal Apple.

The group of studs yells in unison in triumph, drawing my attention back to them. One of them pretends to be shot as another holds his pool stick over his head, announcing, "FNG buys the next round, boys!"

I smile and ask Mick as he pushes my frosted low-ball glass full of ice and golden-colored alcohol across the bar to me. "FNG?"

"Fucking new guy," he explains.

I laugh at the acronym, then look back at the studs. "SEALs?"

"Affirmative. They're just back from a deployment."

I lift my glass and sip the soothing ice-cold liquor. "He looks too young to be a SEAL."

Mick chuckles, "Bella Rayne; I'll let you in on a little secret. The older you get, the younger everyone else looks."

"Apparently!" I laugh and lift my glass in a salute to his wisdom. Then I glance over and study the eye-candy antics as I enjoy my drink. The group of heroes appears to be in their late twenties to early thirties, my age. The only one who doesn't is the FNG.

I smirk at Mick, "Well, I trust he's at least twenty-one...."

He nods.

As I turn to watch them blatantly, I ponder. "Oh, to be twenty-one again."

Mick rejects my wistfulness, "No, thanks! No do-overs for me."

"Really? Come on. Do you mean to say you wouldn't want a redo? Wouldn't you change anything? Do things differently?"

He chuckles at my disbelief. "I didn't say that."

I laugh and spin my glass on the bar mixing the melting ice with the hard liquor. The cubes tinkle against the glass. "I would. I would swear off men altogether and focus solely on my career."

"Bad man, eh?" His eyebrow cocks knowingly.

"Pure evil, Mick." I nod, then shiver. I haven't thought about my abusive past in years.

My former lover, my ex, my number one mistake that cost me my dreams, Manny Morales, wore a three-piece suit like no one else, commanded a room when he walked in, and flashed cash as it came into his possession too quickly. I was fresh out of high school with no hope of affording college, and foster parents who though they loved me, needed my room for the next needy homeless child. I was officially an adult and ripe for the grooming, which Manny did with such skill and finesse that I was completely fooled.

I thought he was an extraordinarily successful young entrepreneur, but it turned out his uncle ran a Mexican cartel. I shiver again and drain my glass, remembering when I accidentally discovered those pictures of the girls bound and beaten on his phone and realized his business was sex trafficking. They were victims who tried to escape. It was like a veil fell away, and I saw him clearly as the devil he is.

He wasn't supposed to return from his business trip to Mexico until after the weekend, so I was surprised when I unlocked the door and found a strange set of keys in the bowl on my foyer table. I hadn't seen a familiar car in the parking lot, but he had an endless supply of different vehicles.

When I entered my bedroom, it was empty. The shower was running. He wasn't expecting me to come home early, or his phone and wallet wouldn't have been tossed carelessly on top of his clothes, lying on my bed.

It lit up with a message; of course, I was curious. He was secretive about his business affairs and guarded his phone. I seized the opportunity to spy on him. I picked it up and read the text. It was in Spanish.

Jefa, putas capturadas y castigadas.

Which translates: "Boss, whores caught and punished." Then a picture came through. The blood drained from my face, and vomit entered my mouth.

Three girls, younger than me, wore metal collars around their necks and were chained together. They were naked, dirty, battered, and bloody. I dropped the phone and took a step back.

Shock turned to terror.

I grabbed my backpack and threw it out of the room toward the front door. Then I grabbed Manny's stuff and ran into the kitchen. I took nearly $10,000 of cash out and stuffed it in my bra. Then I put his phone on top of a burner on the stove, piled his clothes on top, and turned on all of them.

I raced back to the bedroom and locked and closed the door to keep the smoke from reaching him.

Then I grabbed our keys, slung my backpack over my shoulder, and hurried out. No one was outside. I bolted the door behind me and clicked his key fob to find out which was his car. The car parked next to mine unlocked.

I ran to my car, opened my door, and tossed his keys in. I set my backpack on the driver's seat, unzipped the pocket holding my survivors' knife, and stabbed his car's front and rear tires to flatten them. I returned the blade to its holder. Then shoved my backpack out of the way, climbed behind the wheel, and fled the scene.

I turned east out of my parking lot and called my foster brother, Enrique, who worked at the Yellow Rose Equine Therapy Ranch, and asked him to saddle my mustang, Smokey.

When I crossed the river bridge, I tossed my phone and Manny's keys out the window. Then drove to the truck stop and parked my car. I went into the bathroom, changed my clothes, and came out a cowgirl.

I hitched a ride with a trucker to the west side of town and walked the rest of the way to the ranch. When I arrived, Enrique and a saddled Smokey were waiting.

He took one look at me and said, "Don't tell me. I don't want to know. But good luck." Then he hugged my neck, and I rode off into the sunset.

Smokey is the only reason I'm alive today. He

saved my life twice. The first time from falling into a deep, dangerous depression when I lost my family and entered foster care, and the second time, being my untraceable ride out of Texas.

I later changed my name from Allison Girard to Bella Rayne Parker. Eventually, Smokey and I ended up in San Diego and settled down. I figured the West Coast home of the Navy SEALs would be a safe place to establish a new identity. I went to nursing school and love my work in the hospital's trauma unit.

I ask Mick, shifting the focus of the conversation away from me. "What would you do differently?"

"I would realize I wasn't bulletproof." He smirks, then winks. "At twenty-one, I thought I was."

I frown. "You've been shot?"

"In the line of duty. I'm former law enforcement." He nods.

"A cop?"

He smirks, "Secret service."

"Oh wow! That's cool!"

"What are you doing bartending then?"

He grins, "working for tips."

The group of SEALs at the billiard table yells

again, and Mick tosses his head in their direction. "Those guys are the only bulletproof men in the world."

Then he looks down the bar at a man holding an empty glass and tells me, "I'll bring you another after I take care of him." He turns away and walks down to the needy customer.

Continue reading<br>
TARGET BELLA

# Coq Blockers Security Team

**Jeff Crockett, aka Rocket**
Chief Executive Officer (CEO)
Mission Team Leader
Former Navy SEAL Tier One
Special Warfare Operator
Alpha 1
Height: 6'5"
Weight: 260

**Maximus Aurelius Moore, aka Hardcore**
Chief Financial Officer (CFO)
Billionaire Investor
Former Army Aviator
Apache and Blackhawk Pilot

Height: 6'0"
Weight: 200 lbs

### Nina Fox, aka Foxtrot
Chief Operating Officer (COO)
Mission Team Commander
Former Tier One Targeting Officer
For Alpha Team

### Meghan Meadows, aka Ambassador
Chief Liaison Officer (CLO)
Mission Coordination Team Member
Former Army ISA Officer

### Mike Franks, aka Mr. Mom
Mission Team Member
Former Navy SEAL Tier One
Special Warfare Operator
Alpha 2
Height: 6'0"
Weight: 200 lbs

### Jack Black, aka Hammer
Mission Team Member
Former Navy SEAL Tier One

Special Warfare Operator
Alpha 3
Height: 6'1"
Weight: 230

**Jocko Malone, aka Fastball**
Mission Team Member
Special Warfare Operator
Former Navy SEAL Tier One
Special Warfare Operator
Alpha K9 handler
Height: 6'4"
Weight: 250

**Lucifer, aka Luce**
Mission Team Member
Special Warfare Operator
Former Navy SEAL
Belgian Malinois
Multipurpose K9

**Brody Andrews, aka Badass**
Mission Team Member
Special Warfare Operator
Former Navy SEAL Tier Two

Special Warfare Operator
Height: 6'3"
Weight: 265 lbs

**Justin Davis, aka Danger**
Mission Team Member
Special Warfare Operator
Former Navy SEAL Tier Two
Special Warfare Operator
Height: 6'3"
Weight: 230

**Zane Lockhart, aka Insane**
Mission Team Member
Special Warfare Operator
Former Navy SEAL Tier Two
Special Warfare Operator
Deputy Sheriff - K9 handler
Height: 6'1"
Weight: 210

**Batman, aka Bruce Wayne**
Mission Team Member
Law Enforcement
Belgian Malinois

Multipurpose K9

### **Dirk Sam, aka Sam-I-Am**
Mission Air Support Team Member
Former Army Aviator
Apache and Blackhawk Pilot
Height: 6'2"
Weight: 225

### **Micah Young, aka Dark Thirty**
Mission Technical Support Team Member
CIA Agent - Hacker

### **License To Own**
Mission Team Overwatch
Drone Operator
Civilian Video Gamer

### **Nikolai Smirnov, aka Grappler**
Mission Team Hand-to-Hand Combat Trainer
Former MMA Champion Fighter
Height: 5'10"
Weight: 185

### Jessika Klide writing as Stingray23
HOT Military Romantic Suspense

**<u>A Few Good Men</u>**

Target Lizzy

Target Nina

Target Logan

Target Marie

Target Bella

Read Jessika Klide's newest, sexiest, and most talked about bestsellers...

## **LIFE IN LIVE OAK**

*Coming Home For Her*

*Moving Back For Her*

*Opening Up For Her*

*Making Good For Her*

## **SUCH A BOSS**

*Big Book Boss*

*Big Booze Boss*

## **BILLION HEIR**

*Fraudulent Fiancee*

*Escaping in Glass Slippers*

*Accidental Amnesia*

## **THE HARDCORE NOVELS:**
## **SPECIAL EDITIONS**

*Untouchable Billionaire*

*Unstoppable Billionaire*

*Unforgettable Billionaire*

## **THE HARDCORE COLLECTION:**
## **TRILOGY BOXSETS**

*Undeniable Chemistry*

*Unbridled Passion*

*Unwavering Devotion*

## **THE HARDCORE SERIES:**
## **ORIGINAL SIRI'S SAGA**

*Mr. Sexy*

*The Cock-Tail Party*

*Perfect*

*Ladies' Night*

*Battle*

*Sex Pot*

*Heaven*

*Shakeup*

*Hardcore*

*The End*

*Shake Down*

*Family First*

———

Learn more at

JessikaKlide.com

Jessika Klide writing as Cindee Bartholomew

**The Liotine Heir**

American Flyboy

Italy's Most Eligible Bachelor

**Worth The Risk Series**

Secret Life

The Stunning Secret

The Shocking Secret

The Dark Secret

The Twisted Secret

The Startling Secret

*Read in order.*

**Standalone**

Twisted Together

# JESSIKA KLIDE WRITING AS STINGRAY23

writes military, romantic suspense, and thrillers about hot alpha military men and the strong female women they love. These interconnected standalone stories follow a group of former Navy SEALs on missions to rescue victims of human trafficking. Be prepared for a fast-paced, action, and adventure thriller.

Rescues are their expertise. Snatch and grabs are their specialty.

Happily ever afters are their guarantee.

For new release information, sales, and more.

follow on Amazon

or

JOIN STINGRAY23'S VIP READER LIST

https://stingray23.com/

*Stingray23 is the pen name Amazon bestselling author of spicy billionaire romance Jessika Klide. Her husband chose the name when she was inspired to pen a new series about military heroes. He is former military and her real-life hero.

# Jessika Klide

#4 Amazon, #11 Apple Books, and #34 Barnes & Noble Chart Author of character-driven HOT billionaire romcoms Jessika Klide brings readers the perfect blend of heat, humor, and heart.

*"One of my favorite parts is all of the Easter eggs you find if you are a long-time reader of Jessika Klide! If you are on the fence, trust me when I tell you this, just 'Go Baby Go!'"* ~*Goodreads review*

JOIN JESSIKA'S VIP READER'S LIST
for exclusive giveaways, new release information, sales, and more.
https://jessikaklide.com/

Newsletters not your thing?
No worries.

## — CONNECT ON SOCIAL MEDIA —

facebook.com/JessikaKlideRomance
instagram.com/jessikaklideauthor
bookbub.com/authors/jessika-klide
twitter.com/JessikaKlide
tiktok.com/@authorjessikaklide

JessikaKlide.com